Summer CATCH

BETH BOLDEN

Chapter 1

Kieran registered the man sitting down at his bar before he even got a good look at him.

"Just a sec," he called out to the guy who'd wandered into the Pirate's Booty and he'd spotted out of the corner of his eye.

"No rush," a pleasant, amused voice responded. Kieran liked the sound of the voice before he ever saw the man, but even the *feeling* of him was a good one. Like fireflies on a hot summer night or condensation from a cold beer dripping onto his hand as he took a long sip.

Kieran finished stacking the last of the clean glasses from the washer onto the counter behind the bar and turned.

He'd owned the Pirate's Booty before it had ever been the Pirate's Booty. The day he'd bought it, it had been Dan's Bar—such a bland and unimaginative name—but between his bartending job before and purchasing this bar, he'd served probably millions of people.

Every single one of them coalesced into one feeling in his mind. The inevitable tug and subsequent certainty he always felt when faced with someone on the other side of his bar: the knowledge of what they *should* be drinking.

Not what they wanted to drink. Or what they ordered to drink.

But deep down, what they *should* be drinking.

For the first time, that gut instinct was missing. He did not know what *this* man should be drinking.

He looked inside, and that certainty was still gone. The blankness was weird. Unsettling, actually.

The man opposite him smiled. Like absolutely nothing was wrong.

Kieran tried to follow suit. Wasn't sure his smile was nearly as nice.

Because the smile *was* nice. Broad and crinkled his eyes at the corners. Nice eyes, too, a dark, deep brown. Almost the exact same color of the shiny wood bar between them.

Those eyes should have set Kieran at ease. But they didn't.

"What can I get you?" The words were rote, almost a rut worn down the middle of him, comfortable and familiar.

Almost every time, someone gave him a drink order, and depending on who it was, he'd either keep that knowledge to himself, or he'd tell them, bluntly, what they should be having instead.

"Ah, just a beer, I guess. New in town. Not sure what's good." The man offered him another one of those very nice smiles.

"New in town, huh?" Kieran grabbed a chilled glass from the cooler and in a few expert movements poured him a beer from the tap—a tangerine wheat from a local brewery that he liked especially.

Even if he didn't know what this guy was supposed to be drinking, he might as well give him something good. Something cool and refreshing on a hot day.

And it had been a hot one, even for late April.

Kieran set the glass in front of him.

"Yeah," he said. Then shot him a bit of a disbelieving look. Like he couldn't quite believe Kieran didn't know who he was. Not in a smug, egotistical way, but in a *thank God, he didn't recognize me* kind of way.

Kieran had been intrigued before—nobody had ever *not* pinged his superpower like this—but now he was more than a little fascinated.

Kieran looked closer. The guy was young. Maybe just over thirty. And attractive. He rarely noticed that in his patrons anymore because he wasn't the kind of bartender who liked to serve booze to people and then pick them up.

Which had honestly led to a *very* long dating drought and a very intimate relationship with his right hand.

And then it hit him.

Of course he knew this guy.

He'd seen him on ESPN just earlier today, sitting as comfortably in front of a whole wall of reporters as he was now, in Kieran's bar.

"You're the new Condors coach," Kieran said.

"Guilty as charged. Jonathan Kelley." He extended a hand and they shook, Jonathan looking almost chagrined that Kieran had recognized him. "Guess I won't be living under the radar much longer."

"Kieran McDonald. I own this bar. And no, but Charleston's a pretty chill town. We're probably not going to hound you to death."

"Probably," he said with a quirk of his lips.

Kieran shrugged. "We do love our football here. And, before the last couple of years, our Condors."

"Gonna be some big changes." Jonathan nodded, like he *knew* there would be. Like he was going to make sure of it.

But Grant Green, the new Condors owner, had already been around town, making a lot of promises after buying the team, the newest change which was hiring the guy in front of him, so it wasn't going to be entirely up to Jonathan here—but changing the culture was going to be a big part of his new job.

"It's time," Kieran agreed. He leaned forward on the bar. "So, what dragged you in here? I'd have thought you'd be doing something a lot more important than hanging out at the Pirate's Booty." It was still early, and the bar was pretty empty, not surprisingly considering it wasn't quite five yet on a Tuesday afternoon.

"Saw the name, had to check it out—plus I heard some of my guys talking about it, when I met with them. You might know them? Deacon Harris? Jem Knight? Beckett West?"

Kieran nodded. "Yep, I definitely do. Good guys." He said it because that hadn't been universally true for all the players on the Condors. But he'd vouch for Deacon, Jem, and Beck all day long. Even Carter wasn't ridiculous.

"They were saying this was the place to come, and that a lot of the team hangs out here. That you're the owner."

Kieran nodded.

"They ever get into any trouble?" Jonathan asked.

Kieran considered the question. He had a feeling he knew why Jonathan was asking.

"Your diva wide receiver, Carter Maxwell? He makes his presence known, and does his best to pick up everyone in my bar, but other than that, no. They're good guys, like I said."

"That's the vibe I got from them, too," Jonathan agreed. He took a long sip of his beer. "So you gotta tell me, how'd you come up with this whole . . ." He waved around Kieran's bar. The fake pirate propped up in the corner with the semi-molting stuffed parrot on his shoulder. The palm trees. The climbing hibiscus vines up all the exposed brick walls, giving the bar a vaguely tropical vibe.

"The theme?" Kieran questioned.

Jonathan laughed. "Yeah. It's a lot. It's fun, though."

"We also host theme nights. Surprisingly our most popular is Disco Night."

"Really? That's cool."

Kieran grinned back. He didn't know *why* he got such a good vibe off this guy but he did. It felt a bit like his drink superpower, but it was more than that. *Stronger.* Like an arrow that kept pointing unerringly in Jonathan's direction.

He didn't know if the guy was gay. Didn't know if he even liked men. And God knew, the worst person for the arrow to be pointing to would be an NFL coach.

And yet, it kept pointing, anyway.

Well, it could point all it wanted, because Kieran wasn't going to do anything about it.

"You should join us," Kieran said. "You haven't really experienced the Pirate's Booty at its best unless you see it with some neon lights flashing and the Bee Gees playing."

"Gonna be a busy year," Jonathan said, wincing as he offered his excuse.

"I bet." Kieran told himself he wasn't disappointed—but he was, kinda.

Like something had ended before it had even begun.

"Though . . ." Jonathan paused and pulled his phone out of his pocket and set it on the bar. "If you'd be willing, I'd love to exchange numbers."

It was the last thing Kieran had expected him to say. To make an overture *this* quickly? Kieran knew he wasn't painful to look at. Maybe he had his dry spell, but it was out of choice, not because of a lack of offers. But he certainly hadn't expected this.

"Not for . . ." Jonathan laughed nervously. "Not like that. Not that you're not . . .you know. But I'm not into guys like that. Just because my players come here, and if anything happens, I'd rather be your first call, not the cops."

"There's really not anything I worry about."

"Yeah, with the guys you know already, but there's gonna be a lot of new players this year. Ones I don't know."

"Sure. I get it." Kieran shrugged. He'd kind of hoped for more than just *please call me if shit goes down* but it helped to know it wasn't going to happen. Easier to put Jonathan into the friendly acquaintance zone instead of the *want him even though I shouldn't have him* zone.

He recited his number, which Jonathan typed in, and then Kieran felt his own phone buzz with the message Jonathan sent.

"Thanks for the beer, man," he said, giving him another one of those smiles. The ones that warmed Kieran up from the inside out.

The ones that made him wish things were different.

"You're welcome."

Jonathan pulled out his wallet, but Kieran shook his head. "Beer's on the house. As a welcome to Charleston." He grinned. "And hopefully an enticement to come back."

"Thanks again," Jonathan said. He slid off the barstool and gave Kieran a little wave as he walked out the door.

CHAPTER 2

I⊤ should have been easy for Jonathan to forget the oddball bar and the bartender with the stormy gray eyes and blond hair in need of a trim, but it actually wasn't.

After all, he was busy getting ready for the biggest challenge of his career—leading a football team. He'd never even been a head coach in college, only an offensive coordinator, and he knew every eye was on him, waiting for him to fail.

But he wasn't going to fail, because this challenge was not only exciting, Jon already knew it was going to be one of the most important things he ever did.

Even if the Condors lost more games than they won, he'd still chalk up this year as a success as long as the team did it together and did it clean and fair.

Still, even now, late at night, almost midnight by the watch on Jon's wrist, the bar popped into his head.

Every other time Kieran and the Pirate's Booty had entered his consciousness, he'd pushed them both away. Intending to focus on things that were more important.

But not tonight.

Tonight his office just felt a little too cold and a little too empty. Charleston a little too devoid of anyone he could call a friend. From personal experience, his apartment wasn't any better. Not that Kieran was a friend, but he was *something*.

Jon dug his phone out of his pocket, pulled up their text conversation—up until this point, consisting of exactly three words: *Hi, it's Jonathan*—and typed another message.

You never told me why you named your bar the Pirate's Booty.

It was kind of a stupid line, and he'd have been ashamed of it except that he couldn't be, because it wasn't a line. He wasn't trying to pick Kieran up, even as the knowledge of him, all the mysteries contained in those gray eyes, poked and prodded at him.

Jon considered himself an open and fair individual. If he *had* swung that way, he wouldn't have been ashamed of it. Or maybe all that surprised. One of his old friends from high school was gay. His niece was bi, and her best friend was non-binary. He'd easily accepted all of who they were, without question. Just as he'd do to the guys on his football team.

But it had never really happened for him, that gut punch truth that he wasn't just like everyone else. Whatever everyone else was, these days.

He tossed his phone on the desk. Trying to re-focus on the data on his laptop screen, and not on the phone and its unanswered text. Maybe it was too late.

No, that's stupid, he reminded himself, *the guy owns a freaking bar. He's probably part-nocturnal. The way you're gonna be, soon enough.*

Jon wasn't going to be nocturnal. He just wasn't going to end up sleeping much, period. But that was okay, because he could sleep when he was dead, and this opportunity wasn't going to wait for him to get a nice seven and a half hours of shut-eye every night.

His phone dinged. The shit on his laptop screen had no chance against the surprisingly strong pull of desire to look over at what Kieran had sent him back.

If I told you, the message read, **then it wouldn't be as cool.**

Jon smiled, even as he started to type a reply.

That's assuming it was cool in the first place.

Jon was open enough, receptive enough, that he hadn't missed the disappointment flicker across Kieran's face when he'd said he wasn't gay.

Had Kieran *wanted* his phone number for more than just an emergency contact if shit went south?

It was possible.

Ouch, I think my bar's pride is wounded :(

Before Jon could reply that the bar's pride—if bars could even *have* pride—was well-represented by the queer-coded flags hanging by the entry, Kieran texted again.

What are you doing up so late?

That was easy enough. **Always been a night owl. Now I do more than just sit up too late on the couch watching TV,** Jon sent. **Lots of shit to do and not enough time to do it in.**

We both know why I'm up so late, Kieran texted.

You guys aren't busy? Jon wasn't even sure what day of the week it was, but surely if it was one of their more popular nights of the week—or a weekend—and the crowd would be too demanding for Kieran to stand around talking to Jon.

It's a little busy, but I'm the boss so nobody can tell me to put my phone away ;)

Jon knew this was probably flirting, that Kieran was probably flirting with him. He'd seemed like a guy open to the possibilities, with his chill attitude, warm smile, and friendly face.

Then there were all those flags in the entry.

It would be the right thing to do to stop.

To do the adult thing, the *right* thing, and set his phone down, forcing himself back to the work on his screen.

But the pressure of taking this job was never-ending. He never got a break from it. Not for one minute could he forget where this team had been, last year, before it had been sold to Grant Green, a tech billionaire with no experience owning a professional sports franchise. The old owners had been morally bankrupt, ready to drag the whole team and all its players down a desperate black hole of doing *anything* to win a Super Bowl.

Grant didn't want that, and he'd made it crystal clear to Jon that if the Condors did ever win a championship, they'd do so in an entirely different way.

But for right now, one of Jon's jobs was scouting, because money was tight, and it wasn't just about finding great players at a price they could afford, it was about finding *honorable* players at a price they could afford. A much trickier proposition.

Kieran had given him a little bit of respite, for the first time in what felt like weeks, and instead of putting his phone away, Jon leaned back in his desk chair, put his feet up on the edge of the desk, and kept typing.

So, tonight's not Disco Night, huh?

Kieran's response was just as quick. **For someone who seemed unimpressed by the Bee Gees, I'm surprised you even remember.**

Jon laughed out loud. **I'm more of a Donna Summer kind of guy.**

And if he was flirting, well . . .he wasn't stupid. In fact, he'd sort of gotten this job because he'd proven himself to be the opposite. On the football field, anyway. Was he good at relationships? He was fucking terrible at them—when he even attempted them, which was practically never. But he could be a good friend. Even *he*, who worked too many hours, had friends.

Kieran could be a friend that he sort of . . .flirt-texted . . .with, every so often.

No harm, no foul, right?

Now that I can see. You in silver glitter with your hair teased up to there.

Maybe another guy—another kind of football coach, on another kind of team—would be freaked out by the visual that Kieran had provided. But Jon was only amused.

Look hot, do I?

Jon knew he shouldn't have sent it. But he'd gotten into a rhythm, fingers typing almost as fast as his mind was going, and it was too late to pull back, to stop now.

Maybe Kieran wasn't as into this as Jon was, because before, he'd been texting back almost as rapidly as Jon had—but now there was a long, drawn out lull.

A lull that made Jon set his phone carefully on the desk and actually think about what he was doing.

But before he could pull back—or text Kieran an apology for undeniably flirting with the guy, even though he wasn't interested, not like that, anyway, his phone dinged again.

I don't know, I can't remember. Jon made a face, because of course Kieran remembered what he looked like. It had only been a few weeks since he'd been in the bar, and then there was the fact he kept appearing on ESPN. The guy was just fucking with him now, in a way that Jon really found himself strangely enjoying.

He grabbed his phone, clicked the camera, and took a quick selfie, work-mussed hair, tired shadows under his eyes, bad lighting and all. To make it more playful, he stuck his tongue out and made the silliest face he could.

Donna Summer called and she wants her glitter back.

Aw, Jon texted, still chuckling out loud, **am I not fabulous enough for her?**

Not tonight you're not. Get some sleep. Unlike me, I know you can't sleep half the day away.

It was true. He *was* exhausted. He'd been watching film for hours now, and he'd gotten through most of what he'd hoped to, for tonight, so that was just going to have to be good enough.

He stood, stretching out his back, and grabbed his phone from the desk, texting as he walked down the darkened hallway in the practice facility, heading towards the parking garage.

Yes, Mom, I'm going to bed now, I promise.

It should have been kind of weird how Jon had wanted Kieran to tease him again, maybe even pick up on the mention of a bed and use that to flirt with him more, but he didn't. He only replied back: **Night.**

But still, even as he fell into that bed, only twenty minutes later, he realized he was still smiling.

CHAPTER 3

The texting shouldn't have become a thing.

But it became a thing.

Morning, Jon sent a week or so later, **I wish I could hook this coffee up to my veins with an IV.**

They didn't text every day, but when they did, it often went on for hours. Talking about everything and, also, nothing at all. Kieran had friends, friends he genuinely liked—even with his shit working hours—but he'd never had a friend he'd connected to so quickly and so easily. And never like this, with just words.

He'd kept hoping Jon would come into the bar again. But he hadn't.

Kieran was torn about this. On one hand, it was disappointing, because he wanted to know if they had this same easy camaraderie in person. On the other, it was actually a huge fucking relief, because what if they did, and what if it was more—but *only* for Kieran—all the while he knew Jon couldn't possibly like him that way.

How would the NFL feel about you talking so cavalierly about drug use? he texted back as he lay in bed, sunlight streaming over the coverlet.

That'll have to be our little secret.

Kieran told himself firmly that he shouldn't *like* that they had those, now. Even if Jon meant it half-jokingly.

But he really, really liked it.

Liked it enough his cock was already half-hard, both because of his just-awakened state and also because it was hard to help it when he was thinking about Jon.

About his forearms, rippling with muscle. His honey brown eyes. The way he'd smiled.

The undeniably fit body his khakis and polo shirts hid.

Kieran had tried very hard not to think about him in sexual terms. They were *friends*, and Jon had made it clear where he stood, from the beginning. But there was also the matter of how undeniably flirty some of their exchanges got. And how long of a dry spell Kieran was currently in. Both those made it tough to fantasize about anyone else.

Maybe Jon didn't mean for his messages to come across that way. Kieran had sure tried not to take them that way, but it was becoming more and more challenging to stop himself from jerking off while thinking about Coach Kelley in some very explicit terms.

It's been way too fucking long since you got laid.

Then there was that ugly truth.

But even if Kieran wanted to pick someone up, now, there was no way he'd ever be satisfied with that kind of hookup.

An even uglier truth.

What do you think of Landry Banks?

Kieran told himself he was secretly glad Jon had changed the subject.

Shouldn't you be telling ME what YOU think of Landry Banks?

I already know what I think of him. I want to know what you think.

Kieran considered what he knew of Landry Banks, tight end for the Buffalo Bills. He typed the first thing that came to mind, screw the consequences. He blamed the arousal still persistently fizzing through his system, the kind of arousal no amount of ugly truths seemed to kill.

I think he's hot. Good football player, too.

I see your priorities. That your type, then? Big and muscley and built like Thor?

Kieran wanted to tell Jon that *no*, his type most recently had been running to fit, flirty football coaches, but there was no way that wouldn't scare him off.

And damnit, he liked the guy too much to do that, now. Even if it would make everything easier.

Not usually, no. Jealous?

Kieran told himself he shouldn't have gone there. But he was attracted, damnit.

A little, actually. Have you seen that guy? Anyone would want to look like that.

Kieran let out an unsteady breath when Jon's response came in. Easy, breezy, with no hint that Kieran's words had made him uncomfortable.

Right?

He did consider adding more. Something along the lines of, *you've got nothing to worry about, trust me*, but he didn't. He manfully resisted and was proud of himself.

So you think he's a good guy, yeah?

Kieran realized then what Jon was really worried about: if Landry Banks was a good guy.

You'd know better than me. I'm sure you've actually met him. I haven't. Not yet anyway. So tell me, do YOU think Landry Banks is a good guy?

Yeah. Yeah, I do.

Then you gotta trust your instincts. You've got good ones.

You think so?

And *that* was the easiest question in the world, which probably should have made Kieran more worried than it did. **Yeah,** he said. **I really do.**

Then, because it was true, he added: **Well, I gotta get up and supervise the cleaning crew at the bar post-Disco Night. Guess you missed all the Donna Summer again.**

He hadn't been really pushing for Jon to show up, but well . . .maybe he had, a little. How could he stop himself?

Guess I did. Too bad. Tell me, what's the worst thing the cleaning crew's found at the bar?

Kieran laughed as he pushed himself out of bed, groaning a little. He was still hard, and trying to pretend he didn't know the reason why.

Trust me, you don't want to know.

I asked, didn't I?

It was true, he *had* asked.

Well, you can't say I didn't warn you first. It was a diaper. A FULL diaper.

Ew. I thought it was going to be a used condom, or something like that.

Kieran laughed out loud. **A used condom? Oh my sweet summer child, those are a regular occurrence. Thus, why I have the cleaning crew.**

Just for post-Disco Night?

That's usually the wild night, other than the weekends of course.

Kieran popped into the bathroom, peed, brushed his teeth and flipped the shower water on to heat up. When he was out of the shower, there was a reply from Jon.

Are any of your nights NOT wild?

Kieran considered this. **Wednesdays,** he said. He *did* wonder why Jon asked, but when he only sent back a thumbs-up, Kieran wasn't sure what to think. Was he just curious? Or making a deeper point about how busy and popular the Pirate's Booty had gotten? Which...Jon didn't need to. Kieran was very familiar with the rise in popularity his bar was experiencing. Or, the best possibility, which was that Jon wanted to come in on a night when Kieran wasn't too busy to hang out with him?

A few hours later, he was just finishing up the prep for the evening, shoving containers of sliced limes and lemons into the fridge under the counter, when his phone buzzed in his pocket.

Good news, Jon said, **guess who's a Condor as of today?**

Kieran smiled. **That good guy AKA Thor.**

LOL. Yep. Feeling solid about this one.

You should be, it's a great signing. He's gonna fit right in.

Maybe not in the old locker room, but the new one we're building? Yeah, I think so. I thought so this morning, too, but had a momentary freakout.

Are head coaches supposed to have momentary freak-outs?

Shhhh. That's gonna be another one of our little secrets.

Kieran told himself again he wasn't thrilled from the top of his head to the bottom of his sneakers that he and Jon had secrets they shared now—but he knew he was lying.

Someday I'm gonna have enough to get you here on Disco Night dressed up like Donna Summer, he teased.

Someday.

Kieran's pulse accelerated even as he told it, very firmly, to decelerate. That hadn't been a promise. Jon had just been teasing, the same way Kieran had been teasing him. That was all.

Next time you show up, I'm gonna know what you're drinking, he texted, without really thinking about it. Because surely that had to be true. Surely the next time—and there *had* to be a next time, right?—that Jon showed up at the bar, Kieran would look at him and know *exactly* what he should be drinking. His superpower could hardly fail him now, not when he was beginning to know the guy this well.

Except, he'd totally forgotten that he'd never told Jon about it.

You will? *puzzled emoji*

Uh, well, yeah, that's kind of a thing, actually. A superpower thing. MY superpower. Like yours is coaching really great and ferreting out the good guys from the bad.

And it's what exactly? Knowing what a person wants to drink? Like you're a booze psychic?

Uh, not quite like that. More like, people order shit they really don't want, to impress people, or to pretend like they're a different person than they really are. I know what they should be drinking. What, deep down, they really want to drink.

Kieran knew the question was coming the moment he pressed send.

So what should I have had to drink the first time we met? I remember you poured me a beer. A really good beer, actually.

He seriously considered lying—something he didn't want to do, not at all—and telling Jon that yes, that was exactly what he should have been drinking. That the beer he'd poured him had been the one identified by his superpower.

But he'd hardly forgotten, and how *could* he forget, that when Jon had appeared at the bar that afternoon, his superpower had refused to cooperate for the first time ever.

Well. No, actually. Funny thing, when you showed up my superpower kind of went on hiatus.

Kieran winced as he sent the text. Hoping that Jon wouldn't take offense.

What you're saying then is that my general awesomeness overpowered even your SUPERpower?

Ugh. Yes. Sort of.

We're gonna have to try a do-over, Jon replied. **Soon.**

Leaving Kieran half-hard *again*, even though he didn't know what on earth that was supposed to accomplish. He told his cock to stop dreaming, but it wouldn't.

It knew what he wanted, even if his superpower didn't.

How was it going to react when Jon actually *showed*?

And why wouldn't he just tell him when he'd do it? Why leave him in anxious suspense? Prolonging his yearning?

Stupid, Kieran told himself. *He doesn't even know you want to see him. He probably just thinks it's no big deal and he'll stop by whenever he has time.*

Sure, Kieran texted back, playing right along with what he was convinced Jon was doing. Just making it a casual friends-bro thing. That was all.

Chapter 4

Jon knew he should've told Kieran he was going to the bar on Wednesday night. After all, he'd specifically asked the guy which night was the least busy so when he showed up, he'd have a chance of chatting with the friend he'd become so close to over the last month.

But he didn't tell him he'd show up on Wednesday, because Jon knew, deep down, there was a very real possibility he was going to chicken out and not show up at all.

It wasn't because he didn't like Kieran. No. The opposite was actually true. He was afraid he was liking this guy too much. *Way* too much, in a way he didn't usually like guys. In a way he'd *never* liked a guy before.

"Got any fun plans for the night or are you gonna stay here way too late working again?" Oscar, the offensive coordinator, asked him as Jon picked up his laptop from the conference room table.

He and Oscar had just finished another long brainstorming session about what direction he wanted their offense to take, and it had gone on for hours.

So late, he almost told himself that he didn't need to swing by the Pirate's Booty, after all.

But when he finally got in his car, he found himself driving in that direction anyway, his body and his heart overriding his mind. Maybe that should've worried him more, but he found himself drawn to Kieran's bar in a way that defied logical sense.

Jon parked and pushed open the door to the bar and walked in.

It *was* quiet tonight, only a few people scattered around the room, Kieran behind the bar, eyes on his phone as he scrolled through something. Maybe it would be something he'd text Jon.

Except he's not gonna have to do that now. Now, he's just gonna look up at you and say it with that smile on his face and you're gonna . . .

God, what *was* Jon gonna do? Or feel? He didn't know. Maybe that was really why he was here.

He knew the moment Kieran saw him.

Their gazes met and for a second, Jon swore that his heart skipped a beat.

He knew that couldn't happen. It was a scientific impossibility, but he felt it anyway.

"Hey, this is a surprise," Kieran said, a smile breaking across his face as Jon approached the bar. He slid into a seat, the same one he'd occupied last time, and it felt like it had just been right here, waiting for him.

Waiting for him to get his shit together.

Or get your nerve together.

Jon licked his lips nervously. "A good surprise, I hope?" He really should've told Kieran he was coming.

"The best kinda surprise," Kieran said, leaning over the bar. He was wearing an old, faded Condors T-shirt, stretched taut across his chest and his eyes glowed gray and blue and green. A thousand shades, in those eyes.

Jon didn't usually think men were handsome—though it wasn't like he was *against* acknowledging it when it was fact—but Kieran was, plain and simple, fucking hot. Made *him* hot under the collar.

"Are you gonna practice your superpower on me, now?" Jon teased.

Kieran smiled so wide the skin by his eyes crinkled. "What would you say if it's still blank when I look at you?"

What else do you feel when you look at me? Are you trembling inside, now? 'Cause I am. Even though I told you a month and a half ago I was straight, and I thought I meant it.

"Is it? Did I break your superpower?" Jon asked, raising an eyebrow. Aware, on some deep, visceral level that he was definitely flirting with the guy. And not in the vague way he sometimes flirted over text.

This felt like it had purpose.

Weight.

Intent.

Maybe that was why his palms felt sweaty and he was shaking inside.

Because he'd worried it would feel like this when he came back to the Pirate's Booty. And worried that it wouldn't.

Kieran leaned in even more, elbows on the bar. They were only inches away, and that gray gaze swept over him like it could read every single thing he was thinking. Every single thing he was feeling.

"Do I . . .is there something on my face?" Jon stammered.

"Trust me, it's just your face. Maybe I like looking at it," Kieran said, eyes sweeping over Jon. "Thought maybe if I looked at it real hard, something might come to me."

"Oh." Jon swallowed hard. Realized that Kieran was saying his superpower still didn't work with him. *Why? Is that a good thing? What if it's bad?*

But it didn't look bad, with Kieran gazing at him like that.

He'd admitted he liked looking at Jon's face. Was that his way of subtly saying that he found it attractive? That *he* was attracted?

"It's alright," Kieran teased. "I can still make you a mean drink. Whatcha want?"

Jon shrugged. He wasn't a big drinker. Not anymore. Not with this whole team—what felt like this whole city, sometimes—on his shoulders. "Whatever you want to pour me," he said.

Kieran appeared to like that suggestion. He grabbed a copper mug and filled it with ice and, in several shockingly graceful movements, poured in several different things, topping it off with a flourish and a slice of lime, balanced on the edge, before he set it in front of Jon.

"A Moscow mule?" Jon knew what those mugs usually indicated.

Kieran shrugged. "You're tart and a little sweet. Felt like it fit, superpower or no."

"Thanks?" Jon was pretty sure it was a compliment. He took a sip. "This is really good."

"And I didn't even add the edible glitter Carter especially likes," Jon teased.

Carter wasn't here—in fact there were *no* football players here, on a Wednesday—so he felt like he could let out the eye roll that he normally tried to hold back in the presence of the Condors' star receiver.

"Why does that not surprise me?" he muttered.

"He givin' you problems?" Kieran asked.

It felt like the same kind of conversation they'd have over text.

Except Kieran was right there, in front of him, near enough to touch.

No matter how much Jon tried to ignore the thought, he was pretty sure he wanted to.

Not that he was *ready* to. But the desire was there.

"No, not really. Not any more than usual. I worry every time something doesn't go his way he's gonna just lose it." Jon sighed. "I wish there was a way I could help him."

"You gotta wait for him to *want* the help," Kieran suggested, empathy written across his face. "You can't just want it *for* him. And he'll get there. When he comes in here . . .let's just say, I can sense these kinds of things."

"Another kind of superpower?" Jon asked, taking another drink.

"Yeah, sort of. Just a feeling, more than a certainty. Someday Carter's gonna run out of booze he wants to drink and people he wants to fuck."

"God, I hope so," Jon said.

Kieran laughed. And there went that stuttering heart feeling again. In any other circumstance, he'd worry that maybe he was developing a heart condition.

But no, he was pretty sure the cause was *only* Kieran. Like Kieran could be an *only* anything.

"How about you?" Kieran asked offhandedly.

"Am I gonna run out of booze I want to drink and people I want to fuck?" Jon was acutely aware of the fact that he hadn't specified a pronoun this time. Yes, sure, he was technically copying what Kieran had said about Carter Maxwell—who was a *very* open and proud pansexual—but he knew that wasn't *only* why he'd said it that way.

He'd been hoping for Kieran to react. How exactly? He didn't know.

But he reacted alright.

Kieran had been setting glasses up, fresh out of the dishwasher, and the second Jon said it, his fingers slipped. A second later, there was a crash as the glass hit the ground and shattered.

"Shit," Kieran said reflexively, his eyes still not leaving Jon's.

"Uh, sorry?" Jon said.

"Don't apologize." Kieran's voice was muffled as he leaned over and began to clean it up, tossing chunks of glass into a garbage can, but Jon was pretty sure he could detect embarrassment.

Jon saying *people to fuck* had turned the normally graceful and composed Kieran into a guy who dropped glasses.

"Alright, I won't then." Jon took another sip of his drink.

Kieran popped up, still looking a bit flushed. "You can't just say that to a guy," he complained, but the corner of his mouth was quirked upwards into a little grin.

An *adorable* grin.

Jon was charmed, he was amused, and he was more than a little unsettled, deep down. He'd known the evening could take this turn, but there'd been a part of him that had been *almost* sure he'd been imagining it all. That once he was face-to-face with Kieran again, he'd feel the same way he did about so many other male friends of his—platonic friendship only.

He'd never felt that hard yank at the base of his stomach, or any of these butterflies, for any of them.

This wasn't going away. He hadn't misunderstood.

"I take it back," Jon said, trying to keep his voice steady. "'Cause I'm not sure I'm actually sorry."

Kieran's little grin morphed into a full-blown smile. "I don't think you're sorry at all. Besides, no harm, no foul. It was just a glass."

It wasn't, though, not really, and Jon had a feeling Kieran knew it, too.

"The drink's good?" Kieran asked, changing the subject.

Jon let him. Just because he knew what was happening didn't necessarily mean he was ready to talk about it. Nevermind *do* anything about it. Not yet, anyway.

"Best Moscow mule I've ever had, and probably the best company, too," Jon said, honestly.

Kieran gave an approving nod and glanced at a ticket printing out. "I gotta pour this beer, then I'll be right back."

It gave Jon a second to watch him at work. There was a fundamental competency to Kieran's graceful, sure movements that Jon really enjoyed. He could watch this man do *anything*.

True to his word, Kieran was back quickly. "So, you excited for the rookies coming in?" he asked.

"You should ask me instead if I'm ready," Jon said wryly. "Mr. Green's been badgering me to add another quarterback to the roster, give Perez and Charlie a run for their money. I'm not against it, really, but I'm not for it either."

"Why not?"

Jon never felt like Kieran's questions made him defensive. He wasn't asking them so Jon could justify his decisions. He wasn't trying to backseat coach this football team, like it felt everyone else was.

"Nelson's playing well. And," he added wryly, "Randy and I designed a whole offensive system around him. I don't really want do it *again*, if he doesn't work out. I've got other shit to do."

"That's fair."

"Mr. Green just doesn't think Nelson's the future." Jon hesitated and then reminded himself that Kieran was a *friend*. He could be honest with him, and it wouldn't come back and bite him in the ass. "I'm not sure I disagree with him."

Kieran nodded. "I can see that."

"He's . . ." Jon winced. "He's serviceable. He's what we can afford."

"And sometimes you gotta settle for that," Kieran pointed out. "The defense looks good, though."

"They do. We've drafted well the last few years, miraculously." The old ownership hadn't done much else well.

"We're not gonna set the NFL scoring record this season, but I do think we can score some points. Enough, I hope, that we can win some close contests. I'm not hoping for the moon, here, just enough to convince Mr. G to keep me on."

"He's pretty reasonable, though, yeah? He knows the ceiling, considering all your limitations," Kieran said, leaning forward. Those eyes were so hypnotizing Jon wanted to lose himself in them. Forget all about the job he'd been hired to do, the semi-*impossible* job he'd been hired to do.

"He's going to be a great owner," Jon agreed.

"And you, Jonathan Kelley, are gonna be a great head coach," Kieran said with a fierce grin. Almost like he was daring him to argue.

When he'd been hired, *great* hadn't even been on his radar. He'd hoped he could do a decent enough job, with all the cards stacked against the Condors, that they won some games. But more than that, more important than anything else, had been his intention to make sure all his players felt safe in Charleston now. Unlike in past seasons when that hadn't necessarily been true.

"I'm gonna try," he said.

Kieran leaned in closer, so close Jon's mouth went dry—with desire? With want? With something else entirely?

"What I believe is that you're gonna do it," Kieran said. "I've seen a lot of coaches come and go here in Charleston, but there's never been anyone like you, Jon Kelley."

Chapter 5

Kieran knew he should take a step back. Not text Jon so often. Not respond quite so quickly when Jon texted him. There was a very loud part of him that kept screaming he was falling in deep, so deep he might not get out—and how dangerous would that be if he was wrong and Jon hadn't experienced a change of heart since he'd told him two months ago that he was straight?

"Feels like you're always glued to that, these days," Nadia, one of his longest tenured employees mentioned nonchalantly to him, gesturing to the phone in his hand.

Jon had just been telling him about the first day of rookie practice.

They're hopeless, he'd said, **how am I supposed to turn these guys into NFL players? I'm gonna tear my fucking hair out if they don't start LISTENING.**

Don't do it. It's a good head of hair, and it doesn't deserve to be sacrificed for some punk ass kids who think they know better than their coach.

"Yeah," Kieran agreed. He couldn't exactly argue. He knew he should pull back. Try to find a place with Jon that was *just* friendship, but every time the moment came when he should, he couldn't do it.

"New boyfriend?" she asked, raising a dark brown eyebrow.

"No, not really. No."

That eyebrow skated up even higher. "He doth protest too much."

"Hey, Ms. English Literature Grad Student, sometimes an answer is just an answer." He kept his tone light and teasing, but he knew what she was saying. And he felt it, deep down.

What else could he even say? *No, he's just a friend, but I've got a mad, wild crush and I'm beginning to think it might be reciprocated, even though he told me the first time we met he was straight?*

If he did tell Nadia all that, she'd shoot him one of those unimpressed looks he swore she practiced in front of a mirror and tell him if he wanted something, he should just go after it.

But how could he, without pushing Jon into something he'd explicitly said months ago he didn't want?

If things had changed for him, then Jon needed to be the one to say so. Kieran wasn't going to bring it up again, no matter how much he wanted to.

Thank you for always making me laugh, Jon texted back. **Even though it was kind of a weird laugh-crying combo.**

"See there," Nadia said as he glanced back up at her. "I've worked for you for how long . . .three years?"

"Four," Kieran said, uncertain where this was heading, but afraid he knew.

"Exactly. Four years and I've never seen you smile like that at *anyone.*"

"He's a friend."

Nadia crossed her arms over her chest. And then, yep, right on cue was that unimpressed glare. "He's stuck *you* in the friend zone?"

Kieran told himself his ego was soothed, somewhat, by her question. "It's not the friend zone if he's straight."

"Ouch." She winced. "You fell for the straight guy, huh?"

"I—"

But Nadia didn't let him finish. This was exactly why he hadn't told her about Jon before this. "You fell for the straight guy."

"Maybe he's not straight," Kieran said weakly.

"He's not straight."

That comment came from Brock, the new bartender he'd hired six months ago.

"What?" Kieran asked uncertainly.

Then he remembered. Brock had been here the last time Jon had shown up at the bar. The night Kieran had made a total fool out of himself by dropping a glass when Jon had so casually said, *And people I want to fuck?*

He'd forgotten, because it had been slow, so he'd texted Brock to come in late. It had picked up later in the night, but Brock's appearance had overlapped Jon's by at least forty-five minutes. Maybe an hour. Honestly, Kieran didn't remember much about that night except the look in Jon's brown eyes and the way he'd smiled and the way he'd been so undeniably charming. How much Kieran had desperately wanted to slide right over the bar and kiss him until neither of them could breathe.

"I was here, when he came in. That's the guy, right?"

Kieran froze. Jon wasn't just some random guy. He was the head coach for the Charleston Condors. Recognizable. And most definitely not out of the closet, if there even was a closet to mention.

"You see his eyes? I've not seen anyone panic like that in ages. And definitely not boss man here." Nadia gave a confident nod. "That's the guy."

"He's into you, boss. Definitely into you." Brock sounded so sure Kieran felt a surge of envy.

"He's not . . .uh . . .anything. We're just friends."

"Just friends my ass," Brock teased.

"You gonna put the moves on him?" Nadia asked, nudging him with an elbow.

"Uh, no. *No.*" But Kieran knew he didn't sound as sure as he'd felt only a few minutes ago. "He told me the first time we met he was straight. And he hasn't told me any differently, since then."

"Ah, I get it." Nadia nodded knowingly. "You're giving his little bisexual awakening some time to breathe. Smart. Let him come to you."

"What if he doesn't?" The question came out of him before he could snatch it back.

"Aw, honey," Nadia said, her expression growing sympathetic. "It's gonna be okay."

"It's gonna be more than okay," Brock said. "He seems like a cool guy."

Don't say who he is, don't say who he is. Especially in front of Nadia, who will never let it go.

But Brock seemed to understand that he needed to be circumspect, because he didn't say anything else.

"Now that we've had a nice long chat about my love life, who's gonna clean the bathrooms?" Kieran asked.

Nadia groaned and turned to Brock, doing their regular rock-paper-scissors game to determine who had to do the shitty job.

Kieran pulled his phone out again. **Maybe you could stop by again, and laugh-cry in my general vicinity,** he suggested. He hadn't invited Jon to come in since he had two weeks ago, but maybe Nadia was right. Maybe he needed to show a little bit of extra interest.

Convince Jon to meet him halfway.

God, I wish I could. I've been dreaming about your Moscow mules.

Kieran had to wonder if that was *all* he'd been dreaming about. Because a certain coach with kind brown eyes and the kind of lean, tan body he'd love to explore more had been occupying a very central starring position in *his* dreams lately.

Well, the offer's always open.

Maybe next week, Jon texted back. **I'll get a reprieve from all these rookies, and it'll be a week before the veterans arrive.**

Kieran told himself that Jon wasn't putting him off, he really *was* busy. But he couldn't stop from adding another little push. **We don't always have to hang out here, at the bar,** he said, **I can meet you any other time.**

Early in the morning, for breakfast?

Kieran knew he was teasing, because his hours meant that he *never* made breakfast—only brunch, at best.

For you, yeah I'd do it.

Kieran didn't expect Jon to respond to that now or maybe ever, because this was the most obvious he'd been about his feelings.

But to his surprise, Jon texted back almost immediately, before he could even put his phone into his back pocket.

Let me figure some schedule stuff out, and I'll let you know.

It wasn't a *yes*, or necessarily a, *I understand, cause me too*. But Kieran told himself it was something. He didn't want to think of it as a concession, because they weren't negotiating. But it was a branch, extending out, connecting them together even tighter than before.

Chapter 6

Jon was not stupid, and he was trying very hard not to be stupid about this, too.

He couldn't say he had a lot of experience with dating. He'd done it, of course, but nothing had ever lasted a long time. It was hard, when his feelings had never been particularly engaged, not in a serious way, and when he kept moving from place to place, climbing up the coaching ladder.

There was a part inside him who wanted to claim this thing with Kieran wasn't a *dating* thing, at all, but he knew it was a lie the moment the thought crossed his mind.

What he really should do was talk to someone about all these new feelings he was experiencing. Help him parse them out. But the issue with that was he didn't *know* anyone he could ask, at least not well enough to risk revealing so much personal info.

It wasn't like he was an unknown anymore; he was the head coach for the Charleston Condors. He drew quite a bit of media coverage, mostly because nobody knew what to expect from him or his team during the upcoming season. And also, Kieran liked to tease, because he was too young and too good-looking to be the head coach of a professional football team.

If he'd wanted to believe it wasn't like that between *that*—Kieran flirting with him and Jon *liking* it—was enough for him to at least acknowledge that things were changing.

But how to take a step forward?

Jon was out of experience and way out of his comfort zone.

He considered calling his old high school friend, the one who'd come out in college, but they hadn't talked in years, and it would be so awkward for Jon to call him up now. And his niece was too young to give him the kind of practical advice he needed.

He kept coming back to the same thing.

You should just ask Kieran.

But it was *about* Kieran. How could he ask him when it would become obvious, very *very* quickly, that the person who'd jumpstarted all these questions was the man Jon was directing them to?

You should just do it anyway. It's not like he's ignorant. Or blind. Or stupid.

But Jon felt a little stupid.

It was easier for him to keep their conversations light and easy after his trip to the bar. He complained about the rookies. Kieran agreed they were idiots who didn't know their head from their ass.

But even then, even as he kept it light, he knew things were changing.

Kieran was more direct. More undeniably flirtatious. And so was Jon, even as he tried to pretend he wasn't.

You want this. No matter what lies you're still telling yourself.

But it was one thing to want it. Another to acknowledge it. And a whole other to *do* something about it.

In between meetings and practices and convincing the rookies to *attempt* anything he suggested, Jon contemplated the problem.

Kieran had made it clear the ball was in his court.

For you, yeah I'd do it, he'd said about breakfast, only a few days ago. Making his feelings just about as clear as he could.

As clear as Jon had a feeling Kieran felt comfortable with.

It was time for *him* to do something, too. But what?

Jon debated with himself for three solid days before he woke up on that fourth morning and realized that he'd already decided.

He was going to talk to Kieran. If he couldn't, or it didn't go well, then that would be the evidence he needed that they couldn't do this. That they couldn't be more than just friends. But if it did go well . . .then Jon could always make it clear—in case it wasn't clear enough before—that the man who'd led to all these questions was Kieran himself.

And what would happen after that?

Jon felt hot and cold at *that* thought, but undeniably eager enough that he knew it was the right move.

If they couldn't be friends first, *real* friends, who did more than bitch about their day, or celebrate the minor successes, then they couldn't be lovers.

But if they could . . .*well*.

So Jon sent Kieran a text. **I've got a late meeting tonight,** he said, choosing every single word of his text with care. **And it's a Wednesday so I know it's usually light there at the bar. Think you could duck out and meet me for a late-night breakfast?**

He hadn't needed to suggest breakfast—but he wanted Kieran to understand that this was him taking Kieran up on his unspoken offer.

Making it as clear as he could. Maybe not as clear as Kieran had been, a week ago, but, Jon hoped, *clear enough.*

I can do that, Kieran said. **Feeling a breakfast craving?**

If we want to call it that, sure. Jon hesitated. Then told himself that he'd *never* been a coward and to just do it. Embrace it. **And I thought we could talk.**

About?

Jon gave him points for not saying they talked all the time—because they did.

This is why you wanna take this chance. Why you're not gonna duck out on this shot before you even aim. Because think how good this could be, if you had this *and more, too?*

Assuming you had some questions and struggles, too, when you realized you weren't straight.

Jon let out a hard breath. Feeling a little nauseous. He'd done it.

Yeah. Definitely. I'm honored you want to talk to me about it.

He'd already been honest, enough it wasn't so hard to continue.

I wouldn't want to ask anyone else, he texted back. And that was truer than he'd realized, because even if he'd had options, Jon had a feeling he'd have ended up asking Kieran anyway.

Kieran didn't say anything to that, but he did reply ten minutes later. **Rudy's Diner, 11 PM?**

Jon sent back a thumb's-up emoji and they were set for the night.

He didn't want to call it a date—but maybe a *friends but maybe more* meet-up?

Oh, don't be stupid, you hope it's a goddamned date.

He dressed like it was a date. Changing into a different shirt, ditching his khaki pants for a pair of jeans that an old girlfriend had said made his ass look fantastic.

Ignoring the voice inside that insisted, *You can use all the help you can get.*

He got to the diner fifteen minutes early and ordered coffee, even though he was going to be up all night if he drank it.

Or maybe that's gonna be Kieran keeping you up all night.

Jon told himself sternly to stop thinking that way, stop wondering what might happen after this conversation, because if he sweated through his shirt, it wasn't going to do him any favors.

Kieran walked into the diner at three minutes to eleven, his handsome face creasing into a bright, wide smile as he spotted Jon.

"Hey," he said, sliding into the booth opposite him.

"Hey," Jon said, trying not to sound nervous and failing.

"Coffee?" Kieran asked, glancing over at Jon's half-drunk cup. "You got someplace you gotta be after this?"

Yes. In your pants.

"Uh." Jon cleared his throat. How was it possible that Kieran looked even better somehow under these bright fluorescent lights? He'd imagined the impact of him might have been helped along by the friendly dim lighting at the bar.

"Hey, listen, it's alright. I . . .I get it." Kieran's expression turned sympathetic and he reached out, brushing Jon's hand so briefly that, for a second, he thought he must've imagined it.

But he hadn't.

"When did you know?" Jon asked, deciding he was going straight to the question that had haunted him the longest. How had he gotten to thirty-three years of age and not realized he was into guys, too?

It made him feel painfully out of tune with his own brain. His own *heart*.

"Not til freshman year in college actually," Kieran said wryly. "Though—no, that's not quite true. I suspected. But then I made out with David Gardner after getting high at a frat party, and it was kind of hard to deny after that."

"Ah." Jon felt stupid. He'd gotten high at frat parties, too. Never made out with a guy at one. Maybe if he had, he'd have realized this particular truth sooner.

But then if the frat guy hadn't been like Kieran, he didn't think he'd have been particularly interested.

"Listen, though," Kieran said, leaning in, his gray eyes so intent, "sexuality's like a rainbow. Maybe you're red-orange, maybe you're turquoise. Then maybe you meet someone who makes you more of a cobalt blue."

Jon had done some research on his own, and that fit with what he'd read.

"So it's not . . .weird . . .if I thought I was turquoise, but I discovered that I was actually more of that . . .uh . . .cobalt blue? Or even purple?"

"Of course it isn't," Kieran said, sounding so sure that Jon envied him his confidence.

"You're a remarkably judgment-free person."

It was why they'd gotten along so well. Why Jon just plain *liked* him.

Kieran shrugged. Picked up the menu. "It's not that hard to put myself into other people's shoes and have a little bit of empathy for what they're going through."

"And yet so few people do it," Jon said.

Part of him wanted to apologize to Kieran. To say, *I'm sorry, I'm sure this hasn't been easy on you either, because I think you like me, too, and if you thought it was hopeless, that would've sucked.*

But he didn't.

"What are you thinking of getting?" Kieran asked.

"Uh, I don't know." Apparently a theme for the evening. "Maybe the banana pancakes."

Kieran glanced at him over the top of his menu. "I'm gonna get the bacon and cheese omelet? Split with me?"

Jon had already begun to relax, feeling like he'd made the right choice in discussing this with Kieran, but his offer sealed it.

"It's a deal," Jon said. Put his hand out and Kieran shook it impudently, but then their hands both lingered there.

Kieran's calluses brushing the sensitive curve between Jon's thumb and his index finger.

Of course the waitress chose that moment to arrive at their table.

Kieran dropped Jon's hand, so quickly that he wanted to reach out and snatch it back, even though he understood exactly why he'd done it.

The waitress might've recognized him. Might've remembered, later, that he'd been holding hands with a guy.

They ordered, and Kieran added a cup of coffee to match Jon's. "'Cause apparently we're staying up late and playing hooky tonight," he said with a crooked grin as the waitress dropped off a mug for him, giving Jon a refill.

"I'm game if you are." *Please say you are.*

Kieran picked up his mug and clanked it carefully against Jon's. "You know I am," he said softly.

It was the strangest first date Jon had ever been on, and yet also the most comfortable.

After that first initial bit of awkwardness, they chatted so easily, like they had from the first, Jon telling stories about all his idiot rookies and their stupid antics, and Kieran telling him about Brock's first week as a bartender.

"He sliced all the citrus the wrong way, a whole fucking bushel of limes and lemons and oranges, and for *days*, I had to serve drinks with them." Kieran shook his head. "And the second night, he ate a whole jar of maraschino cherries and got sick in the bathroom. All that neon red splashed across the toilet, like a freaking crime scene. But he's shaped up pretty well after that."

"And you could take off, because he's there?" Jon chased the last bite of pancake, scooping it up with a healthy swirl of maple syrup.

He felt jittery and energized, and not just because of the caffeine and the sugar.

He was lit up inside at the thought of what they might do *after* their late-night breakfast.

"Yeah. He's a great guy. Him and Nadia are both easy to rely on. I should do it more."

Jon had never felt the butterflies swirl quite this insistently. After grabbing the check and setting down a few bills, Kieran shooting him an amused glance at his stubborn and determined expression, Jon decided that was the reason that the awkwardness returned.

Should he be the one to suggest continuing the evening? Kieran had made it pretty clear that the ball was in his court. That if he wanted them to move forward, he was going to have to be proactive about it.

What should he say?

We could go to my condo. It's not that far away. Only a few miles away. Then we could . . . uh . . . Netflix and chill?

Except Jon wasn't even sure anyone even *did* that anymore. Would he reveal himself to be very uncool if he said that out loud?

But then to his surprise, Kieran said as they stood up from the booth, "You wanna head to my place? It's only a few blocks away."

Maybe that was why Kieran had suggested the diner in the first place.

Jon nodded. "Yeah. I'd like that."

The air outside the diner was still warm and humid, encasing them in the wet blanket feeling that Jon didn't think he'd ever get used to.

Every once in awhile, a breeze would waft around them and it was so refreshing Jon tipped his head back and let the cooler air sweep over him.

"Not used to the humidity yet, I take it," Kieran teased, watching him intently.

"Not even close."

"Well, hopefully you're around long enough for you to adjust," Kieran said.

"I'm planning on it," Jon said. *Promised.* Trying to say he wanted to stick around and be the Condors' coach, but not just for the team, but for Kieran himself. He'd never connected so strongly and viscerally to someone before. Was it any wonder he was going halfway out of his mind with the thought that in a few minutes they'd be at Kieran's place, in the dark, in private, and nobody would know what happened there except the two of them?

"This is me," Kieran said, leading him up a set of stairs to one of those tall, narrow row houses. But then he stopped at the front door.

"I have to ask," he said, shifting uncomfortably from foot to foot, but his eyes never leaving Jon's, "if . . .well, when we first met you said you were straight and now . . ."

"And now I don't think I am?" Jon asked, and Kieran nodded.

It was the moment of truth. Kieran had brought up the subject, but Jon knew it was up to him to finish it.

"Well, if you're asking if meeting you changed things." Jon reached out and this time there was no waitress to make Kieran pull his hand away. He squeezed it, turning the handshake into something more intimate. Kieran's thumb brushed that sensitive curve of his hand again. Encouraging him, Jon realized. "Yeah. It did. I don't know if it changed me, or I was always like this, and I didn't know, but however you define it, I'm definitely cobalt for you."

"Purple even?" The corner of Kieran's mouth quirked up.

"Bright fucking purple," Jon said. He leaned in and before he lost his nerve, brushed his mouth over Kieran's.

It was different than every other kiss he'd ever had, but *better*, too. The rough rasp of Kieran's stubble, his bigger, broader body, and then there was that undeniable electricity between them that flared to life.

No, he'd never mistake kissing Kieran for anyone else, and yes, he loved it.

Kieran's gray eyes were luminous and filled with happiness when he pulled back. But his arm was still locked rightly around Jon's waist. "Like I said, it's absolutely my honor," he said.

Jon gestured to the door. "You gonna let us in and let me try that again? Cause I have a feeling the second attempt's gonna be even better than the first."

Kieran smiled. "Yeah."

CHAPTER 7

Kieran had been braced for disappointment.

He'd not exactly *expected* Jon to tell him no—there'd been too many things pointing to the fact that he was going to say *yes*—but he'd still experienced a yawning pit of what he *felt* like had to be inevitable disappointment as they'd stood at his front door and he'd asked the question.

But Jon had kissed him instead.

Had gathered what had to be an enormous amount of courage and just leaned in, like he kissed men all the time.

Whoever he *was* kissing, he must have had some practice, because he was really good at it, his lips firm and confident against Kieran's, his body angled towards him, his fingers gripping his T-shirt like he didn't want to let go of him.

But Jon's skill wasn't why Kieran wanted to lose himself in the kiss from the very first moment their lips touched.

No—it was that undeniable chemistry that had hooked him from the beginning, from when he'd looked across his bar and seen Jon sitting there. He'd been caught, even though he'd tried to fight it. Tried to tell himself that it wasn't going anywhere.

But now, Jon was *here*, in his apartment, watching as Kieran grabbed them beers from his almost entirely empty fridge.

"If you couldn't tell, I don't spend a lot of time here," Kieran said as he popped the lids off, setting one in front of Jon, lounging against his kitchen counter, his long, lean body drawing his eye irresistibly.

Jon raised an eyebrow. "And you think I spend a lot of time in my place?"

"Well. No. Probably not." Kieran hated how self-conscious he suddenly felt. Of course Jon didn't care that this place felt like a stranger's house. Jon had been to the bar, which was his *real* home, where everything that mattered lived.

"I think we both work too much," Jon said, sounding amused by this. "Maybe we should try to work a little less."

"Always a good goal," Kieran said. And it was. He did try. But why would he want to be alone in his place when he could be at the bar, with his friends and his employees? Surrounded by the pleasant background noise of his successful business? Maybe if he had someone to share that alone time with . . .

He was still trying to figure out how to broach this subject when Jon set his beer down on the counter with a decisive click.

"You wanna know my goal? I keep wondering how much of this beer I need to drink before I can come up with a reason to kiss you again."

Kieran laughed so hard he nearly snorted *his* beer. "You know, you could just *do* it." Jon was the head coach of the Condors—so confident and in-control most of the time—but he looked downright sheepish.

"I already did it, it's your turn now," Jon said, and he was grinning now too. Probably at how ridiculous they both were, standing here, drinking beers they couldn't care less about, when they could be *kissing* again.

Kieran didn't need another invitation. He set down his beer and walked right over to where Jon was standing. Cupped his face in his hands and kissed him the way he'd wanted to on his front stoop.

Their tongues brushed together as Kieran pushed him up against the counter and they devoured each other. Jon's hands were gentle but insistent as they wrapped around his waist and he pulled him in closer and then closer still.

If Jon was having any uncertainty or second thoughts about kissing another guy, Kieran wasn't aware of it. He'd been hoping to keep some distance because Jon was definitely not used to having a hard dick rub against his own, but the moment he reeled Kieran in close enough to feel it, he groaned in the back of his throat.

That was the turn-on of the fucking century.

If Kieran hadn't been sure this kiss was heading into bedroom territory fast, that would have sealed it.

But one of them was going to have to keep an even head—clearly it wasn't going to Jon, who was kissing Kieran with the kind of all-in abandonment that made him hard as a rock and aching in his jeans. So he pulled back, both them breathing hard.

"Shit." Jon's exclamation was unsteady. His pupils dilated. His fingers tightening around Kieran's waist.

Kieran stroked the back of his neck, the surprisingly soft skin there. "Yeah?"

"Does it make me uncool to admit I've thought about that a lot?"

Kieran chuckled. "Only if it makes me equally uncool to confess that yeah, I thought about it too. More than I should admit to."

"You tried to hit on me the first night we met. Not so much of a surprise."

"Maybe I wasn't hitting on you." Kieran tried to play it coy.

"No, you were. And you should've. I just . . .I got stuck worrying that maybe . . .well, that I was misreading *myself* and then worried I was misreading you, and I didn't want to do that. Not when you'd become a friend." Jon's honesty always blew Kieran away, but that confession made him even more sure that the patience he'd employed, even as hard as it had been, had been the right tactic.

"You had to figure some stuff out. It was okay you weren't sure, right away."

Honesty blazed in Jon's eyes. It was even more beautiful than the honey brown color that had entranced Kieran from the first moment he'd seen it. "In case you didn't realize it, I *really* like you. As a friend. As more."

Kieran had a feeling he should probably be embarrassed at how fast he kissed Jon after that. Or how they stumbled backwards from the kitchen to the living room, Kieran taking the couch and Jon not even hesitating for a moment before he climbed right on top of him.

"This is hot," Jon gasped, one kiss sliding into the next, minutes lost to the scorching give and take of their mouths.

Kieran had given up on trying to keep his cock away from Jon. He was hard. Jon was *definitely* hard, and *God*, had he been hiding *that* under all those staid, Sunday School khaki pants?

He was gonna go out of his mind if he didn't get to see, if he didn't get to touch.

But he wasn't going to be the one to push them further. Instead, he kept to what Jon had established, hands sliding over clothes, exploring each other with long, lingering touches as their mouths fused together.

Then Jon slid a hand right up the front of Kieran's shirt, the sudden feel of skin-to-skin electrifying him, a full-body shiver engulfing him.

"Okay?" Jon asked, pulling back a fraction. His chest was rising and falling and Kieran pressed his palm to his back. Then decided what the heck and slipped it underneath the fabric. Feeling Jon shiver, too.

"You touching me? Always okay."

"I thought this would feel . . . I don't know . . . *weirder*. Unnatural, maybe? And yeah, it's new, but it's really, really good."

"For me, too," Kieran agreed. "But if this is all you wanted to do, that would be fine."

Jon leaned back a fraction more. "Really? If we made out like this for even ten more minutes, I think I'd just combust. Wouldn't be able to help it."

"Oh, there would definitely be combusting happening." Kieran decided he might as well be as honest as Jon was being. "It's been awhile for me. And you're . . . uh . . . pushing pretty much every one of my buttons."

"Can I push them some more?"

"God, please."

Jon pushed his T-shirt up, Kieran helping him the rest of the way, and then before he was even done discarding it, Jon's fingers were at the button of his jeans and he was opening them, like he did this kind of thing all the time.

"Still okay?"

Now that Kieran was looking, okay, his fingers *were* trembling. But that could be nerves. Or arousal. Or both.

"Uh, yeah. Yeah."

Jon grinned, sharp in the dim lighting of the room. He shoved his jeans down and stroked him through the thin fabric of his boxer briefs. Kieran gasped, suddenly and acutely aware that maybe he should have least believed this *could* happen and worn something a little nicer than one of his old pairs of gray boxer briefs. Sure, he'd imagined it. He'd fantasized about it. But he hadn't ever assumed that it actually would.

"You gotta tell me what you like," Jon murmured as he touched him more, stroking and rubbing in a way that had Kieran's eyes nearly rolling back in his head. "I wanna make you feel amazing."

"You are. You definitely are." Kieran moaned a little as he found a particularly good spot, stroking him with more confidence than he'd expected.

"Just thinking of how I'd like to be touched," Jon said.

That made Kieran realize—he could be doing this too. 'Cause he'd definitely thought a lot about touching Jon, and now he could. Free and clear, no worries and no hesitation.

"God, yeah," Jon echoed as Kieran got his jeans partially down and even, *bonus*, his boxer briefs, finally revealing his gorgeous cock.

Long and hard and thick; Kieran's mouth watered at the thought of it. But for now, this would be enough. He began to give him nice slow strokes as Jon tucked his fingers inside his underwear and mirrored his movements.

"Kiss me," Kieran panted.

They leaned together as close as their moving hands would allow and he tumbled right over the edge as their tongues slid together.

"Goddamn." Jon's breathing was harsh as he came down. "*Goddamn.*"

"Good?"

Jon looked him right in the eye. Kieran had a feeling that what he was about to confess might be groundbreaking. "I've never had sex that good," he said.

Yep. Pretty goddamn groundbreaking.

"It was really good for me too." Which was true. Was it the *best* sex he'd ever had? Well, it was certainly up there and considering they'd only given each other awkward handjobs on his sofa, that was saying something.

"Yeah?" Jon's eyes crinkled as he smiled.

"Anytime you want to do it again, I'm here for it," Kieran said, keeping his tone light and his gaze serious.

"How about . . .very, very soon?" Jon asked, his eyes lighting up. He eased back and Kieran could see him looking about for something to clean them up with.

"No arguments from me."

Kieran reached over and grabbed a tissue from the box on the side table, handed it to Jon and then took a few more for himself.

"Hard to believe that was your first gay sex experience. You took to it like a duck to water," Kieran teased as they relaxed back on the couch. And Jon *was* relaxed. Kieran could tell, and he hoped it wasn't just from the orgasm.

He knew, from firsthand experience, how hard it was to fight and fight against something you knew was right, to endlessly debate with yourself if this was *really* what you wanted. Until you got it, and the fight ended in a whimper, not a yell.

In this case, a moan instead of a yell.

"You really think so?"

"I was there. Being the recipient of your first gay orgasm, I think I'm the living expert on the situation, now."

"Good. And you're gonna stay that way," Jon declared. He scooted a little closer. Glanced up at Kieran. "If you're okay with that."

"Very okay."

Jon smiled.

CHAPTER 8

I woke up today and I can't stop smiling.

Jon didn't disagree as he grinned down at Kieran's text.

Then another one arrived, right under the first one of the morning. **Nadia asked me if I finally got laid.**

What did you tell her? Jon asked.

He wasn't upset if Kieran had confided in his friend. But he was also curious what Kieran had said to her. **I told her it wasn't any of her business. But I don't think she believed me.**

Why not?

Kieran sent him a picture then—a selfie, actually—and yes, he was grinning. A big wide smile on his handsome face, and oh yeah, there in the crook of his neck, was an undeniable red splotch on his tan skin. A red splotch that Jon's mouth had made just the night before.

Whoops.

He'd known at some point during the second, lazier makeout session that he'd gotten a little obsessed with the way Kieran smelled and then tasted like, but mostly the way he moaned, deep and resonant, when Jon kissed his neck.

So he'd kept doing it. A lot. He'd assumed he hadn't left any marks, but apparently he'd underestimated his own fervor.

And isn't that the theme of this? You underestimated everything.

How straight you are.

How much you like Kieran.

How intoxicating he is.

Whoops. Sorry.

Don't be. I definitely liked it.

Yeah, Kieran had. Had really liked it when Jon had sucked his neck and gave him another, slower, more deliberate, hopefully *better* handjob.

Then Kieran had slid to his knees and blown Jon's mind with his mouth.

He'd never considered himself sex-obsessed but he kinda was, now.

Couldn't wait another twelve hours before he could see Kieran again.

What else do you like?

Jon was really glad he was in his office, alone, and he was sitting at his desk, because Kieran texted back. **You. Hard and leaking against my tongue and coming down my throat.**

He cleared his throat. Feeling the hard, aching pulse throbbing insistently in his pants.

You're not playing fair.

And you like it.

I love it.

You going hard to your meeting?

I'm TRYING not to but someone insists on tormenting me.

Bad news. We got another reservation for tonight. It's gonna be packed. Not gonna be able to meet up.

Jon groaned out loud.

I know, Kieran texted before Jon could even answer. **I'm bummed, too. But you're gonna still get yourself off. I'm gonna talk you through it.**

Now?

Jon tried to pretend that his heartbeat accelerating was because what Kieran was suggesting was reckless and stupid and he shouldn't do it. But in reality, he didn't think he'd ever been this excited, ever.

He wanted all of this, and he wanted *more*.

You have your meeting, Kieran said, and Jon could practically hear his words in that cute, teasing tone of his. **After. Later tonight. I'll slip away before it gets busy. I wanna talk you through it. I wanna hear you come.**

What about you?

I'm gonna enjoy the hell out of just this. Trust me on this one.

"You ready for the meeting?"

Jon looked up from his phone, feeling flushed and guilty.

"I . . .uh . . .yeah," he stammered.

Randy, the offensive coordinator, had poked his head into his office, and gave him a confused glance at Jon's awkwardness.

"You sure you're okay? Mr. G. saw you *dancing* down the hallway this morning, and now this?"

"Mr. G saw that?" He'd had no idea his *boss* had seen him being so excited about Kieran. Of course, Mr. G might understand, being queer himself, but their focus *needed* to be on this football team. Besides, whatever was going on with Kieran was so new that Jon wasn't ready yet to talk about it.

He thought he would, eventually, but he'd always tried to keep his personal life and his professional life separate. In his opinion, they didn't need to cross. Whatever he was doing with Kieran, as long as it was well . . .*mostly* . . .in his off time, then why did it matter? If he did his job, that was what should matter to Mr. G and the rest of the team.

"Oh, he did. Was laughing about it."

The one positive was that Randy's questions had finally softened his erection. Jon picked up his laptop and his notepad and headed towards the door, joining Randy as they walked towards the conference room.

"I bet he was," Jon said dryly.

"I was expectin' you'd be telling me that the rookies shaped up in practice last night, or something," Randy joked.

"God, I wish," Jon said.

"We'll get them ready."

"I'm glad you're feeling confident about it," Jon retorted.

"I've done this a bunch of times. They always show up thinkin' they know better. But they always fall in line."

Jon knew he was young for a head coach in the NFL, and so it had made sense for him to hire two older men, two much more *experienced* men to be his coordinators.

Randy had bounced around to half a dozen NFL clubs, his innovative offense schemes transforming each team. Jon was an offensive guru himself, so he'd wanted someone who he was sure would never stop pushing the envelope.

Randy had been exactly that guy. He'd been a perfect hire, grounding his staff in his experience and yet fighting for them to be better, to be *different*.

"I'll take your word on that," Jon said. This was such a learning experience. He'd only been an offensive coordinator, never a head coach, and besides, college was different than the NFL, 'cause those guys wanted it so bad, so desperate to keep their scholarships, they'd fall in line. A few of them had developed egos at that point, but they were easy enough to puncture.

But once the guys made it to the NFL, they were given a *lot* of money and had spent the last few years being told by the media and everyone around them that they were hot shit.

It was not quite as easy to puncture *that* kind of ego, as Jon was finding out.

"So, you're not gonna tell me what you were so happy about?" Randy asked when they were almost to the conference room.

"I...uh..." Jon decided he could at least be a little bit honest. "I met someone, actually."

Randy grinned at him. "They make you happy, huh?"

Jon nodded. Happier than anyone else had ever made him. First as a friend, then as a lover.

"Well, I can tell." Randy patted him on the back. "Happiness looks good on you."

"Oh hey, boss, that is a *hickey*," Brock teased as soon as he walked in.

Kieran rolled his eyes. Amused, not annoyed, though.

He knew his staff teasing him was out of love, and frankly, he couldn't even regret it.

"You finally hit that?" he asked as Kieran pulled his phone out of his pocket. Jon had promised to text him when he'd gotten home. When he was finally alone.

It wouldn't be the same as being together. As getting to kiss and touch Jon himself, but Kieran was going to take advantage of every chance he could get.

He was in deep, not just in his friendship with Jon, but the love affair this was quickly becoming.

In so deep, he had no intentions of trying to swim out.

Kieran didn't answer Brock—only grinned, and knew that, coupled with the hickey, was probably enough for him to figure it out.

"I'm ducking out," he told Nadia and Brock. "Hold down the fort."

"Enjoy yourself," Nadia called out to him, shooting him a knowing look.

Kieran shot her an amused glare back.

He didn't pull his phone out and call Jon until he was in his truck, the door locked behind him.

He'd specifically parked in the darkest corner of the lot when he'd gotten back from grabbing dinner at the nearby deli.

"Hey." Jon's voice was already breathless, full of desire.

And you know what that sounds like now. You heard it, loud and in surround sound, last night. You're never gonna be able to forget it.

"God, you sound so hot, all worked up like that," Kieran admitted.

He'd told himself to play it cool.

But they'd made an appointment to have phone sex tonight.

That wasn't playing it cool, at all.

"I am." Jon's voice cracked. "Just thinking about this all day . . .how do people get work done?"

Kieran laughed. "I'm honored. Touched, even."

"Wish I could touch you." This confession sounded wrenched out of Jon's mouth.

"Yeah." Kieran couldn't help himself, reached down and palmed his cock, already half-hard in his jeans, and *yeah*, wished it wasn't his hand, but Jon's. Clever and competent, with those calluses that he was still thinking about.

"You touching yourself?" Jon asked roughly.

"Yes."

"Me too."

Jon's breath came sharper, harder.

"Slowly," Kieran ordered.

Jon gasped, the sound unmistakable.

"Yeah, you like that," Kieran said, and he liked it too. Loved the idea that he was the one giving Jon the pleasure, even if it was Jon's hand on his cock.

"I *love* it." Jon panted.

"You goin' slow?"

Jon made a frustrated noise. It was so hot Kieran couldn't help it anymore. He shoved his jeans down and slid his fingers into his underwear. He hadn't intended to indulge too, but he had a change of clothes in his office at the bar. If things got . . .messy, then it would be okay.

"I like how wet you get." Jon's voice had gone rough but hushed. Reverent. "I want to taste it next time. Taste you next time. The way you did me."

"Shit," Kieran groaned. His cock twitched in his hand, pre-come coating his fingers, just the way Jon had said he liked.

"You'd like that, then?" Jon hesitated. "Even if I was bad at it?"

"Darlin', you could be any which way and I wouldn't give a shit. I just like *you*."

So much for any of the pretense that this was just sex.

"Like you too. So much." Jon gave a hiccupping gasp. Kieran already recognized that sound. Knew Jon was close to coming.

"You're close already?" But he was, too, undeniably. Just hearing Jon's voice shot him right to the edge, especially when he'd been thinking about sex *all fucking day*.

"God, yes. I'm going slow just like you said, and I'm just thinking about your hand being my hand, your mouth, instead, and I have been so fucking close *all day*."

"Yeah. Been thinking all day about sucking you off. About you burying that big cock in my ass. Fucking me until I cry with it."

Jon went silent. Still. Kieran could hear it.

Worried, immediately, that he'd said the wrong thing. Jon was new to all of this. Fucking another man in the ass might be a step too far. Even if he was only doing it in his imagination.

"Shit, shit, sorry," Jon stammered, and Kieran could hear his sharp exhale of pleasure as he came.

"You liked that idea?"

"Uh, *yeah*," Jon said. "You want that?"

"So bad." Kieran's voice cracked. "God, I wanna . . ."

"Come on, baby, come for me," Jon entreated and that was all it took. He was coming, and when he slunk back into the bar, he knew he was smiling even brighter than he had before he left.

There was no denying it anymore.

He was falling, and falling hard.

CHAPTER 9

"WE COULD'VE UH . . .gone somewhere nicer?"

Jon could tell that Kieran was nervous.

The only thing he couldn't figure out was why.

They'd been on dates before. More late-night breakfasts for dinner at the diner by Kieran's place. Lots more phone sex. Even more actual sex.

Jon had discovered that he really loved blowjobs—and not just receiving them.

It had been the most eye-opening and wonderful few weeks of his life.

"This is plenty fine," Jon said, glancing around the little room with its bare wood walls and floorboards, the wiped tables, rolls of paper towels sitting on the surfaces, a substitute for napkins. "I don't need fancy."

"They have the best shrimp in Charleston." Kieran still sounded apologetic.

Dating wasn't so easy with their two schedules—especially with training camp starting for Jon and the bar growing busier than ever. But they were making it work. Still, this was the first night they'd managed to have what anyone else would recognize as a *real* date.

Dinner out at a normal hour, followed, Jon hoped, by sex at one of their places.

Maybe tonight would be the night Kieran finally asked him for what he'd mentioned all those weeks ago—his cock buried in his ass. Jon had *no* complaints about the sex they'd had so far. Even a simple handjob felt better, more satisfying, than anything he'd ever experienced before. He couldn't get enough, and he'd be happy if they *never* did it. But Kieran had said he'd wanted it, and then Jon realized that he did, too.

"For the best shrimp I'd go just about anywhere," Jon joked. "Honestly I didn't even know I was so mad for seafood before I moved here."

"We've got the best in the world, that's why." Kieran's boast was cute, his gaze glowing with fervor. Jon wanted to reach across the table and hold his hand. Switch over to the same side and put his arm around his shoulders. But they were out in public, and Jon wasn't out yet.

"Not just the best shrimp," Jon said affectionately.

Even if they weren't touching, he had a feeling it was pretty obvious that this wasn't just a platonic outing just by the way they kept gazing at each other.

But he wasn't willing to stop looking at Kieran like that—and he certainly wasn't going to ask Kieran to stop, either.

"Aw, you like me," Kieran teased, and for the first time, he did seem more relaxed.

"A lot," Jon agreed.

Kieran's answering smile told him everything that he needed to know. That it was mutual. That he wasn't going anywhere. And that was what made him hope that Kieran had meant it when he'd said he was willing to follow Jon's lead.

You're a public figure and it's complicated for you, I get that, he'd said, a few days after they'd kissed for the first time. *This is on your timetable.*

There was so much going on with the upcoming season Jon had asked, hesitantly, if it was okay if that meant waiting months, and Kieran had just shrugged. *If you're happy, I'm happy,* he'd insisted.

Of course, Jon *wanted* people to know. He'd discovered that desire deep inside himself, already. But he also knew that it was best to be strategic about these things.

He could wait, if Kieran was willing to wait.

"Let me tell you," Kieran said, "the bar was *rocking* when you guys won that first preseason game. You've got the town behind you, for sure."

Kieran didn't need to say, *unlike last year,* because that was just a given. Charleston had hated the old Condors' ownership, and Jon was fairly certain that the feeling had been mutual.

"Yeah?" Jon smiled. "The plane ride home was pretty rockin' too. I don't think anyone expected us to win *any* games."

"You guys are gonna be better than anyone predicts," Kieran promised, even though that wasn't something he *could* promise.

Jon couldn't even promise that. But he could sure as hell put the work in to make it a possibility.

"I hope so," Jon said. The team—specifically the players that had survived Mr. G's purge—had been through the wringer. They deserved some success. And it wouldn't exactly be terrible for him, either.

"Where you guys at next?" Kieran asked, tucking a swoop of honey blond hair behind his ear.

"We're going to Dallas, then Washington. The Commanders. Nelson's finally getting his legs under him. He threw some gorgeous passes to Carter this week in practice."

"Not focusing on the short game as much?" Kieran asked, taking a sip of his beer.

"We are, but why have a receiver like Carter Maxwell and not use him? And that isn't *him* talking," Jon said dryly. It was nice to be able to sit here like this, across from someone he cared about, as a friend and more, and just have a normal conversation.

"Yeah, I can't imagine he liked that game plan much," Kieran pointed out.

"I can handle Carter." He *hoped* he could handle Carter. Carter was notoriously difficult to handle. He'd been on four teams in five years and he'd finally landed on the Condors because they'd hoped his incredible talent would supersede his inability to keep his temper in check or his dick in his pants.

"I know you can," Kieran said soothingly, reaching out and grasping his hand briefly. Too briefly. There were definitely moments he regretted drawing this line.

Moments he wanted to obliterate it entirely.

You will. When it's right. When it's time.

"But at least the defense is solid. I thank God every day that we've got Deacon and Jem, holding down the fort."

"You're not still concerned about that corner?"

"Rex is gonna be okay," Jon said, and it was more of a hope than a certainty—but that was this business for you. Sometimes you could only set things up and hope they worked the way they were supposed to.

"I haven't seen many of them come in yet," Kieran pointed out. "Deac and Jem a few times, grabbing a quiet drink."

"Bless their uncomplicated friendship," Jon said and Kieran laughed.

"Being a head coach isn't necessarily being the best at schemes or game plans or motivation, it's freaking keeping all these different personalities from destroying one another," Jon continued wryly.

"And," Kieran said, leaning forward, a knowing smile emerging, "I bet you're really fucking good at that. In fact, I *know* you're really fucking good at that."

Jon felt the impact of the compliment.

It meant more coming from Kieran because it felt sometimes like he was the only person in the world anymore who really knew him, inside and out.

And still liked him.

"Come on, here's the shrimp," Kieran said, lightening the mood as the waitress set piles of peel and eat shrimp onto their table. "Eat up." His eyes twinkled. "You're gonna need the energy for later."

"God," Jon groaned as Kieran pinned him to the wall just inside his front door and kissed his neck. "I was thinking about this the whole fucking dinner. Ever since you said, *you're gonna need the energy for later.*"

He was already hard and aching in his jeans, so eager for even a touch. Had been that way for what felt like hours now. *Days.*

"Like it when you're like this. All desperate," Kieran teased, lips dipping lower, under the collar of his T-shirt, hands already underneath it, tracing patterns along his chest, his stomach, his abs.

"I like it when you make me all desperate." But still, Jon reached up, stilled Kieran's wandering hands. "Let me suck you."

Kieran half-laughed, half-moaned. "I never imagined you'd love sucking cock this much."

"Me neither." Jon could admit that much, at least, but Kieran didn't stop him as he dropped to his knees, enjoying the view of Kieran's long, muscular legs, dusted with blond hair, and his cock, hard and pressing against the zipper of his shorts.

Jon made quick work of the shorts and then Kieran's boxer briefs, not wasting any time before he leaned in and licked a stripe up the back of his cock. Maybe if he could push Kieran to the edge, to where he was currently living, he'd take pity on him, not drive him absolutely crazy with desire.

"Yeah, ugh, just like that." Kieran's hands settled into Jon's hair, and he didn't pull, but gave a gentle tug. They'd both learned that Jon loved the encouragement to take him harder and deeper, not ever choking him on Kieran's cock, but pushing him right to the edge of his comfort zone.

And Jon not only enjoyed it, he *loved* it.

His own cock throbbed in his jeans as he let Kieran's length slide along his tongue, then farther still, the tip of it sinking into the back of his throat.

He went slow, but deep, and let Kieran feel every inch of it being buried in his mouth. Sucked hard, enjoying the precome that slicked his tongue, eased his way.

There was nothing hotter than this, than making the man he was so crazy about moan and even one memorable time, scream.

This wouldn't be one of those times—they were both too close to the edge already, too long since they last time they'd gotten to do this—but Jon was okay with that.

But before the point of no return, to Jon's surprise, Kieran tugged his hair. Encouraging him to pull back.

"What?" Jon loved the way his voice got rough and desperate when he was doing this.

"Not like this," Kieran said and pulled him, then dragged him towards the bedroom.

There was lube now, in Jon's bedside table, because he'd learned he liked a finger pressing right up against his prostate when Kieran was blowing him. Something, he realized, he could've lived without learning his whole life if he hadn't met this man and he hadn't opened up a whole new world of pleasure to him.

"What do you want?" Jon asked as Kieran pulled his shirt off and finally unzipped his jeans, letting them fall to the floor.

"You, inside me," Kieran said, his own voice equally rough, even though he hadn't been sucking cock.

"God, yes, that, please." Jon grabbed the lube, fingers lingering over the box of condoms he'd picked up a few weeks back in an attempt to be proactive.

"We'll need those for now," Kieran said, shooting him a smile full of promise.

Jon's fingers were trembling as he tried to open the bottle. He'd done his research, of course. He had some idea of how to do this, but the reality was daunting.

"It's alright," Kieran said, comprehension dawning in his eyes. He plucked the bottle from Jon. "We'll do it together."

Jon squeezed his eyes shut, desire rising him in in a hard, inescapable wave. "God, that's hot."

"Even hotter to do it," Kieran said. He slid a finger back, resting right along his hole. Then he slipped it inside and Jon let out a sharp breath.

"Come on," Kieran coaxed, his voice cracking as his finger disappeared farther in.

"Are you sure?" Jon asked and Kieran just laughed.

"Promise I can take it," he said.

So Jon did as he said, slicking up a finger and letting it slide right up against Kieran's.

He was so hot and tight inside Jon swallowed hard. How was he going to actually *do* this without losing all his control?

"Yeah, *yeah*, just like that," Kieran said with a groan as they fucked him, two fingers going deeper and deeper. "Give me another."

"Are you—"

But Jon swallowed his question when Kieran shot him a hot look.

A look that promised retribution if he didn't give him exactly what he wanted.

And while the retribution would one hundred percent be of the sexy variety, Jon still wanted to give his lover everything he wanted.

Carefully, he tucked a second finger alongside Kieran's and as Kieran groaned, slid them in and out.

Too soon, Kieran shuddered and said, "That's good. That's enough. I'm gonna fucking come that's too hot."

Jon gave another thrust and then another, enjoying the faces Kieran made, before pulling out and grabbing the condom.

His fingers weren't just trembling but shaking as he slid the condom on.

"Swear I'm not a virgin," Jon joked under his breath as he positioned himself over Kieran, one of his knees bent back. Kieran's gray eyes were full of love and encouragement.

And heat.

So much fucking heat.

Jon could burn up in all that heat.

"Just like that," Kieran encouraged as he gave one little thrust and then another, sinking into his tight, white-hot ass.

"That feels . . ." Jon felt his eyes roll back in his head. His fingers digging into Kieran's flesh.

"Yeah." Kieran's voice had gone deep and gravelly. "Me too."

"You want more?" Jon panted. He'd gone as slow as he could, but he was definitely reaching the end of his self-control as he bottomed out.

Kieran reached down and gave his half-hard cock a few strokes, and it perked right up. "Yeah." He was breathless. "You're . . .uh . . .big. And it's been awhile for me."

If Jon reminded himself of how tight he was around him, he'd lose it and so he didn't. Just gave Kieran the time he needed and then began to thrust unsteadily. But the more he did, the righter it felt, the *better* it felt.

Half a dozen thrusts later, he was lost to the feel of it, Kieran a vise around him as he moved his own body in tandem with Jon's.

So much of this relationship had been shockingly easy, and so it shouldn't have surprised Jon that this was, too. Felt like they'd been doing it forever, once he'd gotten over his nerves.

Felt like he wanted to do it for the next forever, too.

"Shit," Kieran exclaimed and that was all the warning Jon got before he was clamping down hard on his cock, come shooting up his chest as he lost himself in pleasure.

It only took another half-hearted thrust and he was coming, too, yelping as it felt like he emptied out everything inside him into the condom.

He *wasn't* a virgin, knew his way around the bedroom, even if this was his first time fucking a guy, and he carefully pulled out before collapsing next to Kieran.

Pushed a hand through the sweaty hair falling across Kieran's forehead. "Good?" he asked.

That was the only word in his brain, so it made sense to ask it as a question.

"Really fucking good." Kieran's eyes glowed with happiness. "You?"

"Sure that we're gonna have to try that the other way, eventually," Jon said.

Kieran laughed and pulled him even closer, tucking him underneath his arm.

Chapter 10

KIERAN KNEW THE MOMENT Jon walked in something was wrong.

He was in the middle of pouring a beer and he had five tickets full of Mermaids' Assholes and passionfruit mojitos waiting on him, but he set the beer on the bar and turned to Nadia. "Give me five," he said.

Nadia gave him an understanding nod as Kieran skirted around the bar and guided Jon by the elbow to the end, to a quiet corner. "Hey," he said, "what's wrong?"

"How do you know something's wrong?" Jon asked wryly as he took a seat and Kieran climbed onto the barstool next to him. He only had five minutes—six, maybe, if Nadia was feeling kind—and yet he didn't want to leave until he knew what was going on.

"Your face tells the whole story."

And there it fell even more.

"Perez—*Nelson*—got injured today. In practice. Blew out his knee." Jon let out a breath. "I think he's done for the season."

Nelson Perez was the Condors' starting quarterback and the guy that Jon had spent the last few months building his offense around.

This was a serious blow. And right after they were all beginning to feel like the Condors might defy expectations and be better this year than they had any right to be.

Kieran understood exactly why Jon looked so devastated.

"What are you gonna do? Start Charlie?" Kieran asked, referring to the backup quarterback, who was mid-thirties, a *year* older than Jonathan himself, and had been picked up more to coach Nelson than to actually take the field.

"We *can't*," Jon said, the confession wrenched from him. "Not for a whole season."

"What else are you gonna do?" Kieran knew that money was tight—mostly because they were still paying some of the shit players they'd had to let go for character problems.

It was unfair, but that was the NFL for you.

"I don't know." Jon sighed. "Mr. G has some ideas. Unconventional ideas. But what else can we do? Charlie's great, but he's thirty-five and a better coach than he is a player. He'll even be the first one to tell you that."

"It's not ideal."

Kieran knew how upset Jon was, because he reached out for Kieran, putting a hand on his knee and squeezing.

They weren't exactly *hiding*, but they were still being circumspect. Kieran tried to let Jon set the pace and the tone, but sometimes it was hard. Like this time, when he wanted nothing more than to grab his man and pull him into a big hug.

"You want a drink?"

"Am I still coming up blank?" Jon asked, trying to make a joke and cracking a weak smile.

"Yeah but I got you, baby." Kieran slid off the barstool. "One sec."

"Sorry." Jon winced. "I know you guys are busy."

"Not ever too busy for you," Kieran promised. He looped around the back of the bar and grabbed some bottles, pouring them into a squat glass.

Set it in front of Jon.

"What's this?" he asked.

"Cherry old-fashioned," Kieran said and dropped three—not one, not two, but *three*—cherries into the glass. Only the best for his lover.

He'd give him the whole fucking container of cherries if it would cheer Jon up.

Jon fished a cherry out of the glass and popped it in his mouth. Kieran might've normally made a joke, but he could tell this wasn't the right moment for a quip about popping his gay cherry.

"So," he said instead, "tell me about these unconventional ideas of Mr. G's."

"You know Aidan Flynn?"

Kieran tried to keep his jaw connected to his face. "Aidan Flynn? You mean the Aidan Flynn that's the all-star, Super Bowl-winning quarterback for the Toronto Thunder?"

"That's the one. And no, we don't magically have more room in the budget for a guy like him. But he has a younger brother. Riley. Smaller. Which is why he didn't go in the first round of the draft.

Which is why he's playing in the XFL right now. But playing *lights out*. Mr. G thinks if we don't scoop him up, someone else will."

"And you don't want him 'cause he's what . . .small? How small *is* he?" Kieran had to wonder. If this little brother was *that* good and also had Aidan Flynn as his older brother . . .could he *be* too small?

"He's not *that* small, just smaller than the norm, you know? Maybe 5'9"? But he's *built,* too. As solid of a guy as I've ever seen, and elusive."

"Sounds like you like him," Kieran pointed out.

Jon shrugged. "I *want* to. But then I think of totally re-thinking the offense and I kinda want to cry."

"Would it be that different?"

"Yeah. Riley Flynn can throw, sure, but he can run, too."

"I liked Perez too, but maybe there's an upside here."

Jon frowned into his drink. "A downside, too."

"You can't think of it that way. Sure it might not work out, but think of what could happen if this Riley guy works out? You knew you had a ceiling with Perez, as much as we all liked him. You were designing an offense around him 'cause you knew he had limitations. What if you had a guy with *no* limitations? Where the sky—where your *imagination*—was the limit?" Kieran didn't think he was particularly good at pep talks; that wasn't his forte, after all. He wasn't the football coach. He was just a guy who owned a bar called the Pirate's Booty.

A name he'd only picked because a friend had bet him that he wouldn't dare.

But if Jon needed a pep talk, then he'd do his best.

Jon reached out and brushed his knuckles over the back of Kieran's hand.

"How did you know that was exactly what I needed to hear?" he asked wryly.

"I . . ." Kieran was going to say he'd guessed, because wasn't that what he'd done? But no. That wasn't it at all. He'd *known* Jon needed that. He knew Jon. He *loved* Jon.

"Doesn't matter, actually," Jon said, shaking his head and smiling, *finally*. Because obviously he didn't know what Kieran had just realized. Not what he'd just started feeling, because no, he'd been feeling like this for awhile now. Just hadn't put two and two together until now.

Until he'd looked at this man across his bar and realized that he was the *one*, the one he'd given up finding, sure that his life with his business and his friends was plenty. That he was *happy*. But he hadn't really been, not in the way he could be. Not until he'd met Jon.

"No, it doesn't," Kieran agreed. "As long as it helped. That's all that matters."

Jon took a long sip of his drink. "I shouldn't be surprised anymore, but this is really good."

"You shouldn't," Kieran said, grinning.

The realization he loved Jon had thrown him—but not for as long as he'd expected it might. It had only taken a minute for him to go, *Okay, yeah, I do love him. And pretty sure he loves me too. We're happy. We're gonna be happy.*

"I can't believe your superpower still doesn't work on me. I'm trying not to take it personally."

"I just think it means you're very special," Kieran said. He wasn't ready to say those magical three little words yet—and when he did, he wasn't going to do it with Nadia throwing him increasingly desperate looks every minute or so as an increasingly thirsty crowd gathered.

"Okay. I like that."

"Grab your drink." Kieran skirted around the back of the bar and took Jon's elbow, leading him down the hallway towards the bathrooms and his little box of an office.

Jon barely waited until the door was closed before setting the glass on the side of his desk and cupping Kieran's cheeks in his hands, kissed him hard.

He tasted like cherries and whiskey and the man Kieran loved.

Kieran only had a moment to really feel it so he *felt* it. Lost himself in the feel of Jon's lips on his, warm and insistent, his hands sliding down his shoulders, gripping him firmly, like he never wanted to let him go.

"There," Jon said, finally letting him go, Kieran feeling as wobbly as if *he'd* been the one to drink that old-fashioned. "Now you're properly thanked. Somehow you knew I wanted to do that, too."

"Maybe I just knew that I wanted you to thank me," Kieran said with a low chuckle. "I wish I could stay. I wish I could kiss you a whole lot more, but I've got to help Nadia."

"I know. I appreciate what you *could* do. You're gonna be off late tonight, though, yeah?"

"Yeah." Probably not until two or three in the morning. Far too late to see Jon, who had to be at the practice facility at seven for the start of *his* day.

It wasn't like this was news. Their schedule had been a little tough to figure out from day one. But they'd done it, no complaints, only bringing solutions to the table.

And today wasn't any different.

"Would you mind . . ." Jon hesitated. "I could sleep at your place tonight? I know it's not much, but . . .it'd be something?"

Of course Jon would bring the solution. "I'll only wake you up for a brief peck," Kieran said.

Jon grinned. "Maybe a little more than a *brief* peck."

"I could handle that," Kieran said. Pressed one last kiss to Jon's lips and guided him out of his office, towards the bar. "You sticking around?"

"I'll have a drink or two," Jon said. "I brought my laptop. Thought I could answer emails while I sit here and watch you like a total creeper."

Kieran laughed at that. Had *no* chance at keeping the sound inside. "Only if its mutual," he said.

"It's mutual," Jon said, pressing one last touch to his shoulder, before he had to go disappear behind the bar.

CHAPTER 11

Jon sent him a series of panicked, but then increasingly confident texts about Riley during his first week of practice.

If this fails and he flops and I get fired, I expect you to let me crash in your guest room for free.

Kieran had texted back. **I can do better than the guest room. How about my bed instead? And I'm perfectly willing to accept sexual favors instead of rent.**

Then, the next day. **Shit, this guy can really run. You don't realize how fast he is, because he's deceptively evasive. One moment he's behind the line and the next he's fifteen yards down.**

Kieran had typed out his answer with a grin on his face. **Guess you're gonna have to write him some more running plays.**

Guess I will.

Two days later.

Carter's never been happier. I thought he'd accepted Nelson's limitations, but I guess not. Cause he's fucking thrilled with Riley.

Let me guess, the Condors fans are gonna feel the same.

Then a day later, Deacon and Jem brought Riley into the bar, along with Landry Banks, Beckett West, and a few others.

He got to meet Riley Flynn in person—and when he'd had a second that night, he'd texted Jon. **Met your new QB. He's the real deal, I think.**

You've never even seen him throw a pass. LOL.

Superpower, remember?

That's for booze, not football. Unless there's something you've neglected to tell me . . .

Sometimes it gives me a feeling about people, too. I think Riley's your guy. Same as you're mine.

That what your superpower told you about me? I thought it was conspicuously silent.

About what you should be drinking, yeah. But not about you. I knew you were gonna matter. More than anyone else.

It wasn't saying *I love you*, but Kieran hoped that Jon understood that he was in this, for as long Jon was willing to give him. Hopefully the rest of their lives. Which was why he was letting Jon set the tone on how public they were being about their relationship.

When you believed you had forever, there was no need to rush.

Well, damn. You're cute.

Keep me?

I'm certainly not getting rid of you.

The next day, Jon called him up, late afternoon, and Kieran picked up, Nadia cutting citrus next to him.

"Hey, what's up?" he asked.

"Wanna come to a game?"

"Uh." Kieran hesitated. "This weekend's?"

"Yeah. We have a bunch of games on the road, to start the season, so it'll have to be this weekend. I'm gonna be honest, I kinda want to vomit whenever I think about it. But if you're there, at least once, maybe I won't. Maybe I'll keep my shit together," Jon said.

"Uh," Kieran repeated. He wanted to. He *wanted* to. But Sundays were always busy here at the Pirate's Booty, and he wasn't used to taking that day off, ever.

"You should go," Nadia said, nudging him. "Your cute boyfriend wants you to go to see his football team play? You say yes."

"What was that?" Jon sounded amused. "Did someone just call me your cute boyfriend?"

"Nadia," Kieran said, rolling his eyes, but it wasn't a lie. Jon *was* his very cute boyfriend.

"I know you're busy on Sundays, but I thought, maybe you could get Nadia and Brock to help you out . . ." Jon trailed off hopefully.

"That's what she was just saying," Kieran said, chuckling. "So I think I'll take her up on it."

"Awesome," Jon said. "I'll get you tickets to Mr. G's suite."

"A suite?"

"Like I'd let my very cute boyfriend sit in the stands," Jon teased.

Which is how he ended up, less than a week later, at the Condors' stadium, watching from the owner's suite as Riley and the team ran onto the field.

Kieran couldn't believe he'd lived in Charleston this whole time and never made it to a Condors game, but this was his first one.

And also, his first one attending as a special guest of the head coach.

Of course nobody around him in this luxurious suite knew just how "special" he was—only that he was a friend of Jon's—but Kieran had long ago decided that he didn't mind. That he was willing to give Jon as much time as he needed to work out how to live more publicly.

Seeing all this pomp and circumstance, the packs of media, reporters, and photographers, the attention Mr. G garnered, and the reaction of the fans the moment the team took the field, Kieran began to truly understand the pressure Jon was under. It only made him more determined to give him the space and the time to do what he felt he needed to do.

The suite had an open bar and a large buffet, with everything from hot dogs to fancy Wagyu beef sliders to peel and eat shrimp. Kieran grabbed a beer and a plate and headed towards the front with its two rows of padded seats. He wasn't here to glad-hand and network with all the other bigwig guests of the owner, only to watch his boyfriend and his team.

As Kieran settled into his seat, he watched with dismay as Riley ran back out of the end zone, and the pass he completed was called incomplete. Jon ripped off his headset, pacing back and forth on the sideline, and his heart begin to race as his boyfriend argued with the ref.

But the ref wouldn't change the call, and not only did Riley's great play *not* count, but the Commanders scored two points instead.

Kieran stared at the sideline as Riley looked dejected, Landry talking to him, along with Jon.

God, please let this work.

It wasn't like Jon wouldn't have job prospects if this season was a failure. He was a young, exciting coach. But the opportunities wouldn't be in Charleston, and Kieran wasn't ready to start a long-distance relationship. He *would,* if he had to, but he wanted, more than he'd realized, and not just because of Jon, for him to succeed. Because this city deserved something more than the pain of the old owners. Because this team deserved more, deserved something to hold their head high about.

Kieran had believed this before, but now that he'd met more of the team—Riley and Landry and Beck, and the others—he wanted it for them, even more.

Riley shook off the mistake, though, and Kieran was thrilled to see him play his heart out the rest of the game. It wasn't just him, though. The whole team gathered together and collectively proved that even though they'd just lost their original starting quarterback, they were going places.

After the game, Kieran didn't linger, because he knew Jon would have a lot to do—locker room speeches and then press conferences. Instead, he headed out to the Pirate's Booty, checking in with Nadia and Brock as well as his other employees, making sure everything was good.

Nadia looked up as he walked in. "Seriously?" she exclaimed. "What?"

Nadia rolled her eyes. "What are you doing here? It's your *day off*. You know what that means, right?"

"Sort of?" Kieran shrugged.

"*And*, you're such a sentimental fool," she added, with a smile. "You bought a Riley Flynn jersey?"

Yep, Kieran was wearing the new Riley Flynn jersey he'd bought at the game. It had made sense. He liked Riley so much, and why shouldn't he want to do everything he could to support the guy?

His older jersey was Deacon's, from ages ago, when he'd first been drafted by the Condors, so it had been time to get a new one, anyway.

Kieran shrugged again, flushing a little.

"I guess that's the best way you could buy a Jonathan Kelley jersey without actually buying one," she teased.

"If that had been a choice, I'm sure that would've been mine." Kieran wasn't ashamed of that. How could he be?

"Exactly," Nadia said. And made a shooing motion with her hands. "Now get out of here and go home to your very cute, very successful boyfriend. Celebrate properly, alright?"

"I…uh…are you sure?" Kieran glanced around as he slid behind the bar. "It's pretty busy."

"And," Nadia said firmly, "we have it handled."

"Alright." Kieran knew when it was right to give up gracefully. "Next week we'll talk about a raise. Maybe a manager role."

Nadia's eyebrows lifted.

"You're doing the work of a manager," Kieran said. "And if I want to spend more time with my very cute boyfriend, I'm going to need more help."

Nadia gave him a nod and went back to the drink orders spitting out of the ticket machine.

Kieran pulled his phone out of his pocket as he walked home. **Meet me at my place?** he sent to Jon.

He'd walked the few blocks to his townhouse before he got a text back. **Be there in an hour. Or so. Apparently everyone's decided we're going somewhere after two freaking games.**

It WAS a great game.

After the beginning, yeah. Ugh.

But you guys pulled it off, anyway. You never gave up. Because it's not in your DNA.

You're really missing your calling as a pep talker.

No. Kieran thought about this as he let himself into the house. Caught sight of himself in the hallway mirror in his Flynn jersey. Then he kept typing. **No, I'm right where I need to be. Right where I'm supposed to be.**

And in an hour (hopefully) I will be too. With you.

CHAPTER 12

AN HOUR AND THIRTEEN minutes later, Jon finally pulled up to Kieran's townhouse.

It had been an absolute rollercoaster of a day.

Started out optimistic, Jon excited that Kieran was coming to their first home game, excited *and* fearful about Riley's first start—but then that first play had happened, and Jon had been forced to keep his attitude level, keep his stomach from plummeting to the turf—but then his new quarterback had turned it around.

Had proved exactly why Jon had woken up with his blood buzzing this morning.

It was *still* buzzing, fourteen hours later.

Maybe he should be tired, but all he felt was elation—and an intense desire to finally see his boyfriend.

Jumping out of his car, he jogged up the steps and used the key Kieran had given him to unlock the door.

"Hey!" he called out. "I'm home."

Realized, of course, the second the word left his mouth that maybe he shouldn't have said it that way . . .but then that was how he'd begun to think of Kieran's place, hadn't he? But not just Kieran's place. Kieran himself.

"In the back." Kieran's voice echoed, and Jon realized after sweating it out for approximately point five seconds, he wasn't upset by what he'd said.

Kieran had just *accepted* it.

He walked down the hallway towards the main living space—split between the kitchen and the living room.

The TV was playing ESPN at a low volume, and Kieran was lying on the couch. He lifted his head as Jon walked in.

"Hail the conquering hero," he chuckled as Jon collapsed on the couch, near his head. Kieran lifted it and set it on his lap.

"Hi," Jon said, unable to stop the smile that bloomed across his face. The most authentic smile he'd given all day.

"I'm so proud of you guys," Kieran said softly.

"I'm pretty proud of us too," Jon agreed, reaching up and carding his fingers through Kieran's hair. "I wish I'd been able to see you there."

"Someday," Kieran said firmly, and Jon believed him.

"I'm thinking . . .like the end of the season, and we'll tell whoever you want." Jon *had* worried about this. How could he not?

"We've already done it then." Kieran's voice was drowsy, relaxed.

"Huh?"

"I mean, *you* know. I'd hope you'd know." Kieran turned his head, eyes meeting Jon's, and he cracked a smile. "And Nadia and Brock and a few others at the bar know. That's good enough for me, for as long as you need it to be. Those are the people who matter. I don't need you to get on ESPN or whatever and proclaim your love for me to the sky."

This time it was Kieran's turn to freeze.

Jon watched as panic settled into his gaze—probably much the same as it had Jon himself, only a few minutes before. But Jon had been alone in the hallway then, not facing Kieran.

"Not that you . . .uh . . ." Kieran stammered, trying to continue.

Jon put him out of his misery. How could he do anything else? "I'm not saying I'll never go on ESPN and *never* tell anyone about how much I love you."

"Oh. *Oh.*"

Jon grinned. "Yeah. I love you. Pretty sure you love me too, or you wouldn't have said that."

"I do. I do love you. An embarrassingly large amount." Kieran had the nerve to look apologetic about this, when all Jon felt was pure fucking exhilaration.

Jon's fingers tightened in his hair. "Look at us," he said. "I certainly wasn't looking to fall for anyone when I walked into your bar."

"I was just standing there, waiting. What I didn't know was that I was waiting for you," Kieran murmured.

He sat up and Jon circled his arms around his shoulders, tugging him in close. "Was that why your superpower was so quiet?"

"Maybe I've got no idea what you should be drinking, but I still know what you want. Exactly what you want," Kieran said, the corner of his mouth quirking up right before Jon leaned in and kissed him. It was only a taste, but it was enough to heat his blood.

That was all it ever took of Kieran for him to want, and want *hard*.

"Do you?"

"Oh yeah," Kieran teased.

It was easy to tug Kieran onto his lap. To dig his fingers back into his hair. Kieran's breath stuttered as his pulse accelerated.

"Show me," Jon whispered and Kieran did. Kissing him long and lush, his tongue swiping against his own.

It was quick and it was slow. Jon needed him *badly*, his cock pressing hard and insistent against his zipper, but they had all the time in the world, no need to rush, no need to not enjoy every blessed second, so he didn't rush.

Kissed Kieran over and over again, sliding his hands over his T-shirt, under it, feeling every inch of his skin, *loving* every inch of it.

Kieran gave as good as he got, restlessly pressing his body against Jon's, like he couldn't get close enough.

When they finally broke apart, Jon was panting, the sound harsh in the quiet of Kieran's place. "I love you," he said, because now that he'd said, he couldn't *stop* saying it. Because he did, so fucking much.

Kieran leaned in, resting his forehead against Jon's. He could practically taste his lips again. "I love you, too," he said. "And God, I want you."

"Yeah?" Jon slid a hand down, gripping the irresistible curve of Kieran's ass.

"God, yeah." Kieran exhaled sharply. "*Please.*"

Jon tucked a hand down his shorts, the muscles underneath his touch tensing and then releasing. Ghosted just a finger down his crack, to his hole. Felt it flex as Kieran's head dropped to his shoulder and he mouthed at his neck.

"Shit," Jon groaned.

"Come on, babe, I gotta have *something*," Kieran said. He reached over and grabbed the lube from the drawer next to the couch, handing it off to Jon as he wiggled his shorts off.

"You're too good at that," Jon chuckled, slipping his finger, wet with lube, back down, Kieran groaning right into his ear as he began to work it in slowly.

"And you're too good at that," Kieran retorted, his voice full of sexual heat.

"Had a good teacher."

"Ugh, just like that." Kieran's voice stuttered as Jon found the spot inside him that always made him breathless, always made him lose it.

Because it didn't matter how many times he'd made Kieran moan, he wanted a hundred more. A thousand.

Wanted to hear his breath catch every day for the rest of his life.

"I know how you like it, babe," Jon murmured. "Just like that. Oh yeah. *Yeah.*" Felt his cock twitch at the thought of all this tight heat wrapped around it.

"Give me another then," Kieran begged.

He had every intention of giving Kieran everything he wanted—everything he needed—but he wasn't going to rush anything.

"Just enjoy it," he said, thrusting deeper, twisting his finger around. Taking his time. Glorying in that heat, before he slipped another in.

"Fuck," Kieran muttered.

Jon pressed in slowly, feeling every inch of Kieran's body as it sucked him in. His cock was wet against his shirt, catching on the fabric.

Kieran reached down and wrenched his T-shirt off, throwing it on the floor. Began to ride Jon's fingers as his cock pushed, damp and rock-hard, against his stomach.

He knew Kieran could come just like this, two or three fingers in his ass, his cock pressed against his skin.

But he wanted more than that. Wanted to be buried so deep he didn't know where he ended and Kieran began. Craved that closeness.

"One more," Jon insisted, finally tucking his third finger in. "Come on. Work for it, babe. Let me know how much you want it."

"Want you," Kieran panted. His fingers tightened on Jon's shoulders. "Want you so fucking bad."

"Gonna have me," Jon said, his own breath not so even.

Wishing that he'd had the forethought to shed his pants before they'd gotten in this position.

"I got you," Kieran said and moved enough to dislodge Jon's fingers, sliding down to the floor, gorgeous and boneless as he reached up for the belt holding his cock back.

Jon groaned as Kieran divested him of the rest of his clothes and then leaned in, giving his already aching cock a long, tantalizing suck. Leaving him wet and wanting.

"Get back here."

Kieran didn't need any more encouragement than that. He climbed back on Jon's lap and then, positioning his dick against his hole, began to sink down.

"Goddamn," Kieran groaned. "That's so goddamned good."

It was better than good. It was fucking heaven, being inside Kieran. Even having to resist moving, when he wanted to desperately, was amazing. Just sitting here and letting Kieran take as much as he wanted was better than any sex he'd ever had.

"Good?" Kieran teased as the backs of his thighs finally met Jon's.

"Shit, yeah," Jon said and reached up, cupping Kieran's neck, tugging him down so their lips met again.

Kieran gave an experimental thrust, moaning into his mouth. Jon thrust next, and then they were moving together, wild and uninhibited and messy. Like they'd already been waiting too long.

"Love you," Jon groaned into Kieran's neck, wrapping his arms around his back and pulling him in more insistently. "Love you all the time."

Tensing, Kieran thrust one last time and clenched down, his cock unloading on Jon's stomach as he rode out his orgasm. Pulling Jon right into his, body milking his come out of him.

They collapsed onto the sofa.

"We're gonna make a mess," Jon said a minute later. It had been really good, leaving the condoms behind—there was *nothing* like Kieran's heat searing him with nothing in between—but it *was* messier.

"Don't care," Kieran said drowsily. "Eventually we'll burn this couch and buy a new one. Won't stop us from fucking on it."

Jon held back in the chuckle—if he did laugh, the mess would inevitably be worse.

"I love you enough I'll even go couch shopping with you."

Kieran opened one eye and pinned Jon with a look. "If you're gonna fuck me on it, you can participate in the buying."

"Fair," Jon agreed and risked reaching down for Kieran's T-shirt, using it as a stopgap measure as he carefully slid Kieran off, cleaning up as best as he could.

A few minutes later, they were curled up on the other end, avoiding the wet spot.

"Am I gonna get that kind of welcome every time we win?" Jon teased.

Kieran smacked him on the shoulder. "Maybe next time I'll just let you suck my cock, since you love it so much."

He couldn't really argue with that, because he did.

Instead, something he hadn't really expected to say came out. "I thought we were done, after Riley ran out of the back of the end zone, today," he admitted. "I shouldn't have felt that way, though. Shouldn't have even thought that."

"You were afraid. It's alright. I was fucking terrified," Kieran agreed.

"But you're not his coach."

"No. Just the coach's very cute boyfriend," Kieran inserted.

"Sometimes I feel like I've got all this shit figured out, and then something like this happens, and I realize, *not so much.*"

"You're giving your guys room to fail and room to grow and room to succeed. To *win*." Kieran partially sat up now, pinning Jon with a very serious look.

"I want to win, for me. And for them. Mostly for them."

"Me too, I think," Kieran agreed. "For this city. You're the best thing that's happened to us in a long time."

"Just to the city?" Jon questioned.

Kieran laughed. "Me too. But then you already knew that."

"Guess I did." The long day was finally beginning to catch up with him, and Jon was suddenly having trouble keeping his eyes open.

"You know what I did after that happened with Riley?"

"Cried? Wondered if you were gonna end up following me to Green Bay or LA or Seattle?"

"Went out and bought a Riley Flynn jersey."

"Oh." That wasn't what he'd expected Kieran to say.

"Best way I could buy one of yours. 'Cause he's your guy, now, you know?"

Jon did, now.

"Yeah," he agreed. "And so are you."

Epilogue

Ten months later

"I do love a wedding."

Jon shot Kieran a heated look as they took in the crowd scattered across the country club field. "Oh yeah? You've only said that about a hundred times. And that's just in the last few days. You tryin' to tell me something?"

Kieran grinned. "I said it plenty of times when these two tied the knot the first time."

It had been during the Condors' bye week. They'd been sitting out on Kieran's terrace, sharing some beer and enjoying the sunset, when the text had come in about Beck and Micah.

In fact that was what Kieran had said. "I love a wedding," he'd proclaimed.

Jon had not felt so positively about it.

But then Kieran hadn't spent the last few weeks trying to prevent his second-year safety, Beckett West, and the newly traded corner and Beck's ex-best friend, Micah Rose, from killing each other.

"Guess murder wasn't on their minds after all," was what Kieran had said next.

And well. Jon couldn't really disagree with that assessment, even though, before that text, he'd been *very* sure that was the case.

"You did," Jon agreed. "There was a reason you were willing to indulge all of Carter's bachelor party planning."

"It was the big fat wad of cash he gave me," Kieran said, but he was smiling. Besides, they both knew the money had had almost nothing to do with it.

"Next you're gonna tell me that falling in love has made you a romantic."

"Lie. I was *always* a romantic. Just didn't have an outlet for it," Kieran said. Reached out and took Jon's hand. Squeezed it. Because now he could. Because they were doing this, now, officially, in *public*.

They'd agreed that Beck and Micah's wedding reception would be their first appearance together.

The season was over, the Condors making the playoffs despite nobody believing they would, and Jon knew it was time.

To Kieran's credit, he hadn't been angry or upset or happy. When Jon had suggested they go to Micah and Beck's wedding reception together, he hadn't even looked surprised—or hurt or upset or any-thing else—he'd just asked when they were leaving.

Jon squeezed Kieran's hand back. "You want a drink?"

"Sure, but I think the resident bartender should take care of our libations, tonight," Kieran teased. "Make sure the staff here is doing their jobs right. You go mingle."

Kieran must've caught a glimpse of his panic. "I'll be back, no worries. You're not gonna have to make small talk alone."

"Sure, alright."

He'd just watched Kieran wander in the direction of the bar when Grant walked up.

"Jonathan," the owner of the Condors said, reaching out and shaking his hand. "Good to see you here."

It had been a long season, and somehow, in the middle of it, the owner had gone from Mr. Green to Mr. G to *Grant*. Now, Jon counted him as a friend.

"Couldn't have missed it."

"I'm sorry—did *I* miss something? You were just standing there, uh . . .holding hands with the bartender from the Pirate's Booty."

Jon grinned. "You didn't miss a thing."

"So when you told me you could date someone and nobody would know . . .that was from personal experience." Grant looked like he was trying to process this news in real time, and despite his very big brain, he wasn't doing a very good job of it.

"Yep. For about a year now."

"The whole season?" Grant's jaw dropped.

"Yep," Jon repeated, nodding. "I'm assuming you don't mind."

"How could I?" Grant retorted wryly. "When the entire world has spent the last few months completely obsessed over *my* relationship?"

Jon laughed. "I appreciate you taking all that heat, so the rest of us could continue to do whatever we wanted, under the radar."

"You're welcome," Grant said. "But really. I *am* happy for you two. He seems like a good guy."

"He's the best," Jon said simply.

"Carter says he pours the best Mermaid's Asshole, but I guess we'll take *that* endorsement with a grain of salt."

"If you've never had a Mermaid's Asshole, then you're missing out," Jon teased.

Grant looked skeptical.

"Mr. G! And Coach!"

Speak of the devil, there was Carter Maxwell in the flesh, walking over, hair even blonder in the bright sunshine and a wide smile on his face.

"Carter," Grant said, the corner of his mouth quirking up.

"Good to see you," Jon said, nodding at his star wide receiver.

"Apparently I've been missing out," Grant said.

"On?" Carter sounded really curious now. Which was a dangerous state, but they'd managed to navigate a whole season without Carter blowing up—in fact Carter seemed like he was happier than ever, with the team and with his own boyfriend.

"I told him he needed to try a Mermaid's Asshole," Jon explained.

"Well, if Kieran doesn't *tell* you to drink one, then you can't," Carter said very seriously, very earnestly. "I tried to order one once without his approval, and well, I regretted that. A lot."

"Noted," Grant said. But he turned to Jon then, and he already guessed what the owner was going to ask.

"So what do *you* drink?" Grant asked. "Since you're dating the bartender with the superpower, I'm sure it's something good."

"What, *wait,*" Carter exclaimed. "You . . .and *Kieran?*"

"Oh yeah." Jon tried really hard not to laugh at Carter's outraged expression. The man thought he knew *everything*, but that wasn't even remotely true. "Actually, apparently his superpower doesn't work on me."

"*What.*" Carter continued to look blown apart.

"I know, it's such crap," Jon said.

"What's such crap?" Kieran walked over then, carrying two drinks.

A beer for himself, and well, whatever he'd ordered Jon, he knew it would be good, because the man had never poured him a bad drink. Even when it wasn't him doing the pouring. But they were all different. Always different, in fact. A kaleidoscope of different drinks.

"What's this?" Jon asked him as Carter's jaw continued to drop farther with Kieran putting his arm around his waist. Like he'd been doing it this whole time. Like he was *born* to do it. And maybe he was.

"Pomegranate martini."

"Him . . .*you* . . .together," Carter stammered.

Jon had never seen him, not once, at a loss for words, so he was going to enjoy this while it was happening.

"You alright, Carter?" Kieran asked, also grinning like his whole day had been made.

"I'm . . .re-aligning my whole universe," Carter said.

"Sounds challenging," Grant said, laughing as he patted him on the shoulder.

"But you're gonna be equal to the challenge," Jon said firmly.

"Oh yeah. I'm just . . .what *is* your drink?" Carter spluttered.

Kieran looked at Jon, his gray eyes very warm, full of love. "He's all the drinks, Carter. All of them. Every drink in the universe."

Comprehension dawned on Carter's face.

"Good for you two," he finally said.

"Come on, Carter," Grant said and took his elbow. "Let's go find Ian."

"Ian. Yes. *Ian*." Carter muttered his boyfriend's name as Grant dragged him off.

Jon laughed as they walked off. Turned to Kieran. "That was a really good line. You been practicing it for the *many* questions were gonna get about me and your superpower?"

"Actually," Kieran said, leaning in and brushing a kiss across his cheek, "it's only the truth. You couldn't just be *one* drink, I realized. You're all of them. Every mood. Every feeling. Everything I'll need."

Love billowed inside Jon. "You *are* a romantic."

"Guilty as charged."

To read or listen to the completed Charleston Condors series, click here.

NEW OWNER. NEW COACH.
NEW PLAYERS. NEW RULES.
BUT ONE RULE HASN'T CHANGED:

THE STAR - DON'T HOOK UP WITH YOUR BEST FRIEND'S LITTLE BROTHER.

THE GAME – DON'T MARRY YOUR EX-BEST FRIEND IN VEGAS.

THE SCORE – DON'T SEDUCE YOUR AGENT-APPOINTED C*CKBLOCKER.

THE PLAY – DON'T FALL IN LOVE WITH THE OWNER OF YOUR FOOTBALL TEAM.

WWW.BETHBOLDEN.COM/CONDORS

INTERESTED IN READING MORE OF
BETH'S BOOKS?

CHECK OUT A FULL LIST OF TILES
BY SCANNING THE QR CODE
OR VISITING HER WEBSITE

WWW.BETHBOLDEN.COM/BOOKLIST

www.ingramcontent.com/pod-product-compliance
Lightning Source LLC
Chambersburg PA
CBHW070354310726
48977CB00002B/434